Dominique Fabre

# The Waitress Was New

Translated by Jordan Stump

*archipelago books*

English translation copyright © 2008 Jordan Stump
Originally published as *La serveuse était nouvelle*
by Librairie Arthème Fayard, 2005
Copyright © 2005 Libraire Arthème Fayard

First Archipelago Books Edition, 2008

Library of Congress Cataloging-in-Publicaton Data
Fabre, Dominique, 1960–
[Serveuse était nouvelle. English]
The waitress was new / Dominique Fabre ; translated by Jordan Stump.
p. cm.
ISBN 978-0-9778576-9-2
I. Stump, Jordan, 1959– II. Title.
PQ2666.A215S4713 2008
843'.914–dc22      2007036286

Archipelago Books
232 Third St. #AIII
Brooklyn, NY 11215
www.archipelagobooks.org

Distributed by Consortium Book Sales and Distribution
www.cbsd.com

Printed in Canada

Jacket art: *Max Jacob (1876–1944)*, Amedeo Modigliani, 1916. Oil on canvas.

This publication was made possible with support from Lannan Foundation,
the National Endowment for the Arts, and the New York State Council
on the Arts, a state agency. The work also received support from the French
Ministry of Foreign Affairs and the French Cultural Services in the U.S.

Oh yes! I hated Sundays,
Because that's the day when I think
And count the days past and to come.

*Pierre Morhange*

# I

The waitress was new here. She came out of the underpass and hurried down the sidewalk, very businesslike, keeping to herself, as tall as me even in flat-heeled shoes. Maybe forty years old? That's not the kind of thing you can ask a lady. She had a sort of flesh-pink makeup on her eyelids, she must have spent a long time getting ready. I didn't look too closely at her shoes, the way I usually do to size someone up, because I had a feeling she'd seen some rough times, and there was no point overdoing it. And I've seen some rough times too, I tell myself now and then, but

I'm not even sure it's true. The sky was all cloudy. Sometimes, on gray days like this, you can see why you're here, in a café like Le Cercle. People come in to get out of the weather, they have a drink, and then they go on their way. The boss was smoking his morning cigarillo when she showed up. He and I got along nicely, I think you could put it like that. I'm already about to retire, whereas he's in his prime, theoretically, but he has problems with his cholesterol, and other health worries besides. He keeps his pills in a corner of the bar next to the Casio. I used to have to take the same kind myself, and I'm still here, but I think that sort of got to him, he seemed a little on edge. Sabrina hadn't been in for three days now, she'd sent a note from the doctor, she had a bad flu. The new girl must have been wondering if this was the place, I wasn't sure if she was going to come in or keep walking. The boss was dreading another lunch shift alone with his wife and me, and without Sabrina, and of course it's not easy finding someone who knows the job to fill in just like that.

The boss threw her a quick glance, she took her little piece of paper from her purse and came in, slower now, yes, it was her. He didn't budge, he just put down his smelly cigarillo in the green and white Suze ashtray. We don't get much call for that kind of apéritif anymore, but we still have the ashtrays with the name on them. We also have Dubonnet glasses here at Le Cercle, and other kinds with the brand names of bottles that never come down from the shelves, maybe they still mean something to the customers, what I don't know. She looked a little nervous, and I gave her a big smile to encourage her when she came up to introduce herself. A lot of the time the boss has a sour look on his face, kind of like a bulldog, but he's not such a bad guy, really. Sometimes he'll sulk for two or three days, even a month or two, and then as quick as it came over him it's gone, and that's the end of it. That week he was scowling more or less full-time, and had been for almost a year, but what can you do, that's the boss. She said something to him in a quiet voice, I couldn't hear because there was a garbage truck being loaded outside. I could see two little green men with big gloves on their hands, along with a mattress done in by the rain yesterday and the day before. I'd already looked at that mattress a couple of times, I'd even made a quick detour to walk past it on my way in, it spoiled my view. I wondered if somebody was moving out, or maybe there'd been a death, unless someone had just left it there because they'd got a new bed. There's a big furniture store not far from here, on the pedestrian street. It was a king-size, with the usual stains, all on the same side, and little feathers that hadn't felt a raindrop for a good ten years. I've slept alone for too long. I've never even had a chance to try Viagra, which apparently works wonders, and ends lots of marriages, from what I hear in the café. I'd like to, from time to time. Hundreds of bottles went tumbling into the truck when the dumpster lid opened, and it made one hell of a racket, if you'll pardon the expression. But of course everybody has to throw out a mattress sooner or later, and if you're still alive your nights will never be quite the same. The trashmen shoved it in on top of the bottles and drove away. That would have made a good commercial for Alcoholics Anonymous, I thought to myself, but that's not my line of work. The trashmen go to the other bar, across the street, La Rotonde. I have no idea why it's called that.

The boss shook her hand and introduced me. "This is Pierre," he said, and she gave me a nod, her eyes were sort of small but bright, maybe because of the cold outside, it was nine-thirty in the morning. I put out my hand and said "Hello, how's it going?"

What I really wanted to say was "Welcome to the club," and then give her some tips on the questions she was probably going to ask. The boss isn't much of a talker, but he's him and I'm me. I'm only the oldest employee of Le Cercle, which is the café where I work, across from the Asnières train station, where there's nothing to see but people coming in and going out, trains every seven minutes to and from Saint-Lazare in Paris, and also some double-decker Transiliens to Argenteuil, Versailles-Rive Droite, Versailles-Chantier, Évreux, Dreux, and lots more places in the outer suburbs. She had a firm grip, when she let go I noticed she had a big wedding ring on her left hand, and I wondered if that's really where it's supposed to go. That was all too long ago for me, maybe I'd forgotten. Still, I'd stayed married for eight years, I was a young man then. I kept my ring on at first. Then I put it in my nightstand drawer. I lost a lot of illusions, but not her. My ex remarried, lived happily, and had two children. Then unhappily, and still two children. Then we lost touch. Her name was Marie, like my adoptive mother. The boss looked around, he'd picked up his cigarillo again.

"Well, let me show you the kitchen," he said to Madeleine.

With a jerk of his chin he pointed me toward a customer who

comes to see us three times a day, I won't mention his name out of Christian decency, he's overdue on his tab. The boss had already asked him more than once when he'd be paying, but last night at midnight, apparently – I'd gone home a good while before – the guy had suddenly burst into tears. He'd undone his necktie, laid his suit jacket beside him on the bar next to his final drink, and the boss had had a terrible time getting him to stop his little strip-tease. He was undressing to go throw himself into the river "in the altogether," as he put it, the Seine's just two hundred meters away. Not even that. I went over to him, I held out my hand, and he gave it a gentle little shake. "Hello, Pierre, how are you?" It's always the same, once or twice a week he goes on a bender at Le Cercle, then the next day he's all sweetness and light. Sometimes I had to see him home. He lives on La Lauzière, which is a little uphill street not far from the train tracks, where you'll find a few millionaires' villas, his among them.

"So, feeling fine?" I asked.

He seemed a little out of it, which gave me a chance to look toward the station. The mattress was gone. "Yeah, I'm doing OK. Thanks." He's a developer, he's in on all the crooked deals that go down around here, I've even been told he knows the people on the District Council, all those suit-wearing lowlifes from Neuilly,

Levallois, Clichy, and Paris-La Défense, but then people tell me a lot of things. I listen, but I don't really hear. I put some coffee in the Lavazzo machine, because I knew he'd be wanting a cup at this time of day, and then I came and bent down beside him.

"You're going to have to pay us, you know," I said, with my hand in front of my mouth so no one could hear.

The boss doesn't like dealing with that sort of thing, especially with a guy like this. Also, he's too quick to lose his temper. The guy looked at me, he's one of my favorite customers here, deep-set eyes, never a pain in the ass, a cup of coffee between nine and nine-thirty, daily special at lunchtime when he's not away on business, and then for the past few months he's been coming in after work, too, when I'm finishing my shift. Sometimes we talk, which for a barman means I listen while he throws out sentences that don't always know where they're going, about his life, his career, his children. He has three, with three different wives. The oldest of the girls is thirty, and he's just turned sixty. They look a lot alike. Sometimes they eat together at Le Cercle. She's a psychiatrist at Marmottan Hospital. She must be his favorite, I've never seen the two others. Does she know her daddy makes a habit of undressing in Le Cercle to go throw himself into the Seine when he's had one too many? I don't think she has the slightest idea. I like seeing the two of them here, sometimes I even have regrets.

"Oh lord, I really tied one on, Pierre! Can you get me a glass of water?"

He took out a tube of Nureflex with codeine and dropped two tablets into the glass.

The new girl was already setting tables back in the dining room. There's nobody here in the morning but the kids from the high school, usually just two or three of them, this is where they come to skip class. They don't always have enough cash for a Coke, or even a coffee. I'm well known around here, they call me by my first name, I can't always keep them straight but generally it's a pleasure to see them. We also get people waiting for a phone call to set their course for the day, and housewives from the villas behind the train station, they come in together for a cup of coffee before they head off to the shops. He gave a big sigh and asked what he owed us. Without my noticing, the boss had left by the back door, next to the old dumbwaiter from before they renovated the café. Sometimes he uses the front door like everyone else, but now and then he slips out on the sly. They live above Le Cercle.

"Hang on a minute, if you don't mind, I'll go see," I said.

I went to the Casio and found his sheet under the coins. He hadn't paid for ten days or so.

"160 euros," I told him.

I didn't ask if he wanted to check over the bill, because with the states he got into, he'd have no way of judging. He pulled out his Société Générale checkbook, then said "No, not that one" and got out another, from Barclays. He filled out the check with a fancy Mont-Blanc pen, the slender kind, like the one the boss's wife keeps in her purse to sign the vendors' invoices. "Thanks," I said, and I set down a change saucer beside him. That made him smile, not really a nasty smile, just a smile.

"Do you want a receipt?"

"Yeah."

"I'll go write it up."

"I don't know if I'll be back for lunch."

"We have lamb chops with ratatouille."

"Right." (He was looking toward the train station.) "I'll see. Could you please put this on my account?"

"No problem, have a good day."

He put on his jacket and got out his cellphone. His workday was starting, it was after ten.

"Thanks," I said, picking up the twenty euros he'd left as a tip. He paid those all at once too.

He was a prince of a customer, the boss would be happy.

I went on serving drinks, soon the lunch crowd would be trickling in, I had a little chat with the new girl, she lived in Paris on the Rue David-d'Angers. She asked if I knew the neighborhood. You bet I did, I'd spent a good twenty years knocking around Buttes-Chaumont. I'd done some short stints at a big café on the Rue Manin, just left of the town hall. Ah yes, she could picture the place. She knew her way around the nineteenth arrondissement. There was still room for people like her there, and in any case she lived alone. How would she fill her spare time if she didn't live in Paris? She was born on the Place Colonel-Fabien. For the past three years she'd been living across from the swimming pool on the Rue David-d'Angers.

"How long does it take you to get here?"

She also casually asked me how business had been, and I was happy she'd come to trust me so quickly, I'm a fixture around here, people realize that. I served a few beers, brought the schoolkids their coffee, two coffees plus three glasses of water, and the girl greeted me with a peck on the cheek. "What's new, Pier-rounet?" As usual, I wasn't thinking about anything much. I was wondering why the boss had left without a word, and even that didn't particularly interest me, in the end. I was just feeling a little disturbed by a dream I'd had the night before, and not for the first time, either. Here I am nearing the end of my working life and I still have dreams about my job, sometimes they terrify me, I'd like to understand that. This guy had come in with another guy, they looked at their watches and changed their minds, it was too early to serve them anyway. They turned around and left without so much as a word to me, and mind you these guys had to be in their forties. I wanted to give them a piece of my mind, but I kept quiet. The new waitress went into the kitchen for a chat with Amédée, the Senegalese cook we found, he's one of the best the bosses have ever had. They even gave him a raise to keep him around, but I don't know if that's going to do it. I went in to see him as soon as I got here, just like I always do, once I've wiped down the bar to start off my day. We talked for a while, that Amédée knows a lot of things. He rents an apartment in Saint-Denis, by the new tramway line. I used to go visit him on our days off back when I had my Renault 5. By bus it would take me an hour and a quarter at least, maybe even more with the changes, and that's too long. We call each other "my friend" when no one's around to hear us, and not as a joke, either. The new girl would fit in nicely, I was sure of it now.

I spared a thought for Sabrina, who'd been a real ray of sunshine around this joint these past few months, thanks to the big smiles she gave the customers and the good times she had with her two children, which she was always happy to tell us about. She loved taking the kids' pictures. She got on well with the boss's wife, too, or at least she did at first. Madeleine had put the napkins into the glasses with the kind of artistic fold you can't master without some sort of experience. Apart from the fact that on the whole I didn't give a damn, the day was off to a good start, the boss still hadn't come back. His wife always shows up at eleven o'clock sharp. She stopped coming in earlier after the renovation, when they redid the café and we stopped selling tobacco and candy and little cards to scratch at or fill in or peer at from under your glasses while you check a tiny TV screen over the bar, and those Morpion cards with the little bugs smiling at you, or sneering, try again tomorrow. It really wasn't worth the trouble, there are two other places to buy that sort of thing right nearby, there's a newsstand and a big Relais H for smokes, and then another one at the other end of the underpass, a little hole in the wall where they don't serve food. Now and then the new girl looked at her watch, she took off her apron, and meantime I'd got everything on my end ready to go for the next three hours, which are always the toughest in this business. At times like that, when you've got to be serving the meals, and making sandwiches for the people who only want sandwiches, and making sure not to mix up the office workers' apéritifs, and doling out coffees and after-lunch drinks all the while, you're a long way from the realm of psychology, which is really the most important thing in a barman's life, after all.

At eleven Amédée came out of the kitchen to ask me if the boss's wife would be eating with her husband. I'd have my meal later, about three in the afternoon, he'd be sure to set a daily special aside. I thanked him, and then I served the first apéritifs. The phone rang as I was serving a kir royal to a salesman from the Neubauer car dealership, he'd just closed a sale, he'd got a certified check for 42,000 euros and was buying his buddies a drink to celebrate. I caught myself smiling as I overheard his story, how he'd reeled in the customer after just three meetings, and as for the car I bet myself he'd be telling them all about it in the five minutes to come. That was a favorite topic of conversation around here, and then for the past few years there were cellphones and computers, too. I'd stopped before then. Would my life have been better if I'd been able to buy that kind of car? At least I was in no danger of breaking the speed limit. I was in the booze business, and those two don't mix well, if you don't mind my saying. I dried my hands and picked up the receiver, I could hear the noise from the train station, which is easy to ignore except between noon and three. I'm a little hard of hearing in my left ear, even though I was never much of a masturbator. I have troubles with my memory too, but anyway. I said "hello hello hello" ten times or so, someone was making a crackling noise on the other end. Where was he? It was my beloved boss. He had a problem, was it serious? "No, it's OK . . ." Anyway, I didn't hear the whole thing, and he asked me to tell his wife to come down now, he wasn't going to be able to get back. I bit my tongue to keep from suggesting he do his dirty work himself, and like any barman who knows his job I didn't ask why he wasn't calling her on their private line. I'd noticed he had his glum face on this morning, and the sullen way he was smoking, but I didn't think it was that bad. He'd already pulled this stunt once, back before the renovation. He was the restless type. He'd stayed away for three days, which completely did us in at Le Cercle, and then he came back fresh as a daisy.

"Got it, boss."

"So everything will be OK?"

That's what he wanted to know, now the connection was clear, I realized he was in a car, somewhere somebody honked at him. He sounded like a little kid caught in the act.

"No problem, we'll manage."

"How's the new girl?"

I looked over at her, without meaning to. She was smiling at Amédée through the pass-through, he hadn't started hitting the beer yet, but he would once she turned in the first orders. You might have thought she'd been here for centuries, except she wasn't yet forty.

"She's great, she's a pro."

I must have been a union organizer in another life, because apart from a guy called Bruno who screwed everything up around here, in the bar and the dining room and the kitchen, with his asshole ways and his secret love affairs, we've had nothing but good workers at Le Cercle, the boss, his wife, and me.

"Terrific. See you later."

"That's right, boss, nothing to worry about."

I hung up.

I thought about my dream again, but I didn't have time to go into it because sometimes we get a big rush all of a sudden. There was a nip in the air outside. Usually the office workers spend their food allowance in the bakery next door, making sure not to go over their limit, but sometimes they come here for a hot dish, especially when the weather's bad. I don't look outside too much because everything that matters to me in life always ends up sitting down at my bar, but just then I had a feeling, and I looked out toward the street. Yes, it was going to rain. Now the office workers sitting on the benches across the tunnel with a novel or magazine might be coming in, and then there were also the guys from the new Monsieur Meuble furniture store, they always took time for lunch, you'd think they had no idea that the people who were at that same spot before had all gone off to sign up at our wonderful local employment agency. I say "wonderful" so as not to demoralize the French family, and also because I've been there myself. I served a young couple, they looked like lovers to me. "I'll have a small scotch, what about you?" "Me? Same thing."

And then the woman changed her mind, she was a petite blonde in high heels and a pink jacket with a scarf knotted over it, still tanned from the summer that had been over for two months now. On second thought, she wanted a Coke. Then I got the usual "small beer, no head" from a young guy who often came to Le Cercle, dressed all in black, his nose always stuck in a book, a collection of poetry in paperback, and other sorts of books too, he covered them with gift-wrap, and I'd concluded they were either valuable or smutty. Of course, they've got videos for that sort of thing nowadays. I always tried to make out the titles when his back was turned. No smut there. Which didn't particularly surprise me, to tell the truth. Sometimes I bought myself a copy of one of his books at the new bookstore on the Rue Maurice-Bokanovski, just out of curiosity.

"Thanks, Pierre."

"You bet."

I saw him almost every day. All in all, he seemed like a kid who needed a blowjob and then a Mars bar, or maybe even both at the same time. What will you have done with your youth, my lad?

Now I could feel cold sweat trickling down from my armpits, I made change for a guy who often came in for a cup of tea, he'd asked for a glass of water so he could take some pills, completely bald, white pants, pit-bull neck, and half-moon glasses on a silver chain. "Thank you sir, have a good day." Alopecia, that word came to me all of a sudden, because of the crossword puzzles I do. My last girlfriend got me started on those, and I've grown very fond of them now that I'm alone. He nodded, and my thoughts turned to cancer. I tried to switch to Kojak instead, but not for too long, those were bad times when I watched Kojak on TV. Madeleine was standing by at the ready. She kept a professional smile within easy reach of her lips, she'd redone them now, I like that little face they make just afterwards, that little pout to even out the lipstick. I told Amédée the news about the boss. I'd see to the sandwiches, along with Madeleine. He looked at me, his hands busy with the whipped cream for the desserts, and gave me a big African frown, he was very interesting to look at.

"The boss isn't here, his wife's not here, Sabrina's not here! What the fuck is going on in this dump?"

Our cook liked to curse, like most cooks, come to mention it, I'd figured that out little by little in the various places I've worked. I didn't answer. If you asked me, he was the best cook in Asnières in our price range, and the fact that the boss was gone wouldn't

‹ 24 ›

change anything on the other side of the pass-through. Amédée always yelled at him too when he tried to come into the kitchen. Only the boss's wife was allowed, as long as she didn't touch anything. I went back to the bar, things were going to get rough if she didn't come down in the next half hour. I told the new girl it was going to be a hard shift, the boss had got held up at the last minute. She shrugged, I guess she was feeling sleepy.

"What's he up to? Where is he? Do you know, Pierrounet?"

I wasn't supposed to know, so I raised my arms toward the ceiling. I was just about to call his wife when she came in through the front door, much to my relief.

She'd been looking younger and younger these past few weeks. I didn't much care why, professionally speaking, but I had an idea. She greeted the customers at the bar on her way past, she even gave the lunch tables a quick scan, like a radar sweep, and she went straight in to say hello to Amédée, he's the first person you have to greet in a café-restaurant, because it's the cook that counts at this time of day. Still, I was second in line, and then she went over to the new girl with a big smile, she gave her one more briefing, and they seemed to respect each other completely, two old pros in the restaurant business and love stories gone bad.

Sometimes, on special occasions, we'd say hello with a quick kiss on the cheek.

"So, Pierre, everything's going well?"

"Yes, just fine."

"Where did he go, he's not here?"

"He called, he got held up."

"Oh, I see."

Even with her beauty-shop UVs, I could tell that came as a shock. She was already turning on the Casio, it was noon sharp. It's always rush rush rush with people around here, when what we all really need is more time. Three tables filled up, two four-tops and a three, Madeleine went by with the menus, then back with the apéritif orders. The boss's wife put down her purse behind the cash register, where we each have a little spot for our things under her watchful eye. I was sorry not to have had five minutes to myself like I try to find every day before the rush starts, I would have splashed some water on my cheeks, I would have drunk a little bottle of Perrier, and I would have tried to put on a proper barman's face.

I've been fifty-six for three months now. My last birthday didn't really get to me, but my fifty-fourth almost threw me into the

Seine, if you'll pardon the expression. I took a half-day off to see a prostate specialist and get my free checkup from Social Security, they couldn't find anything wrong. That filled me with joy for two days, just long enough to pick up a nasty hangover. I thought about my dream again, then pushed it away with a shrug as I served a beer-and-Picon to a guy from the MMA insurance office on Maurice–Bokanovski, he has a pointy beard and a black suit, Sabrina calls him Landru. And after that I just kept right on going. Fortunately the new girl knew her job, because without the boss around it was hard work manning the bar. Amédée was in his unusual good mood, and Madeleine had to get after him a couple of times, nothing terribly serious, but the pass-through's too small, the dining room was noisy that day. The boss's wife wasn't letting it get to her, she stayed behind the cash register the whole time, looking like she was thinking of something else, probably wondering where he could have got to, and keeping an eye on things like she always did, between chats with the regulars. Once or twice I caught her giving the ceiling a blank stare, the boss had it repainted two summers before, during the August closing. Since I hadn't gone away on vacation that year – or the year before or the year after, for that matter – he'd asked me to keep tabs on the work, and I did. She had the dreamy look of a boss and wife whose marriage was heading steadily downhill, if you asked me.

"Pierre, two coffees for table six! Pierre, a carafe of Côtes du Rhône, two carafes of water, a small Vittel!"

All that to be served chop-chop, with all these people lined up in front of me at the bar, I don't really know them but I've been serving them day after day for a good thirty years. At one point, when she didn't have a bill to ring up or change to make, the boss's wife left her post and hurried out to Le Cercle's front door, to see where the hell he was, I suppose. I didn't need to look out to know he wouldn't be coming. No one in sight but the train-station crowds and the office workers, and of course the bums, of which we had our share around here after noon, and some-times till late at night. Then she shrugged, as if she was all alone, talking to him, and went to put fresh cloths on the free tables. She was quicker about it than he was, but usually that was his department. He knew how to give the place a certain ambiance, and how to keep the customers coming back, even if fidelity's not really his strong suit, I'm just throwing that out.

My bar was full from end to end, and, as happens from time to time, depending on the month and the year, I felt a big wave of fatigue washing over me, sweat was trickling down my temples because of the heat from the kitchen. Amédée caught my eye, I brought him a beer, and there was a problem at the pass-through, yet another, Madeleine had burned herself on a hot plate.

"Can't you be a little careful, for Pete's sake?"

He didn't answer. He grumbled something or other. The boss's wife came back to the cash register with a frown on her face.

"What, she doesn't know how to pick up a plate without burning herself?"

Jolly times among the crew, and with no boss there to help us, what's more. I let her little remark go by without comment.

Then, just as quick as they'd come, the customers went on their way. At last I could go to the bathroom, with all the fuss today I hadn't had time before the rush. I took care not to look at my barman mug, but it never fails, somebody opened the door while I was washing my hands, and by reflex I caught a glimpse of his face and my own in the mirror over the sink. Time to change the towel, it was starting to get grimy, and it's little details like that that distinguish a high-class establishment like Le Cercle from an ordinary suburban café-restaurant. My eyes were looking a bit red, but the main thing was that for a few weeks now, I think, I've been seeing some new crow's feet at the corners, and all of a sudden I was afraid. I might not be up to this job for much longer, but then how could I live? I had to take care of myself. Once the other guy was gone I took a moment to give myself a closer look, on top of everything else I'd left my comb in my jacket on the door by the old dumbwaiter, I was looking a little mussed, and I didn't like that. Still, we'd done good business today. The place across the street gave us plenty of competition, but thanks to our cook, and also, I think, to my skill at listening to people talk about everything and nothing from behind my bar, and thanks to our regulars, who don't see much of a difference between here and there, we were hanging on. It wasn't that easy, according to the boss. Sometimes he sat down with his account book at a table in the back of the dining room. He smoked a cigarillo, sharpened a pencil, and started punching numbers into a calculator with an inspired look on his face, like a schoolkid waiting for recess. He'd sit there for an hour or two, getting more and more discouraged. His wife signed the checks, generally. I was going to have to go looking for him, she was waiting for lunch to be over to bring it up with me. He'd had some flings these last few years. She was more discreet about it. The fact is that turning forty had really got to him, and then, with their only daughter gone to England for a year, the two of them must have spent every evening sitting around looking at each other, I understood completely.

I was feeling better when I came out of the bathroom, I'd found a little time to get myself back in working order, and in half an hour or so the hardest part of the day would be over. Madeleine was leaning on the bar, smoking a cigarette and chatting with the boss's wife, she was telling her where she'd worked before. She lived on the Rue David-d'Angers, and the boss's wife asked why she hadn't found work closer to home.

"Oh, I don't know," the waitress answered. "Why not? I like to get out, it's no trouble."

"Is that right?" The boss's wife was surprised. "But doesn't it take you a long time to get here? And what'll you do if they pull one of their strikes?"

I shook hands with a few regulars I'd got to know over the years without really trying to. They're here, they come in for a drink, a bite to eat, they read the bar's newspaper. They never forget what they are, or all the things they have to do, but for a few minutes, maybe an hour or two, they put themselves between parentheses, and I bear the name of that thing in their lives. There was also Henri, my boss, and his wife Isabelle, but she tends to keep to herself. Once or twice a week she went to run errands in Paris, she always took her day off on Wednesday, hairdresser and beautician, sometimes she went to the movies, then came back at six in the evening. As for him, he was never away from his bar for too long, but just lately, after his first disappearances, he'd taken to slipping out through the back door and wandering off hither and yon, not just in Asnières but also in Colombes, Gennevilliers, Courbevoie, like he was looking for something he'd lost. But what? I had no desire to try worming it out of him. We all have our job to do. Soon I was going to have to go see what was up. It bugged me having to do that, because I'm just an employee here, in a way.

Outside I saw a pretty woman walking along with a big red umbrella under some not very threatening gray clouds, the usual early-November drizzle. Her hair hung down to her shoulders, ruffling in the wind. There were already more than a few dead leaves, the city workers had neatly pruned the sycamores on the square but they still make dead leaves. She looked in my direction, but of course it wasn't me she was looking at, and came into the café. I couldn't have been happier to see her.

"Hello, and what may I do for you?"

I like saying stupid little phrases like that, just to put people in the mood.

"A coffee, please."

She had a very gentle voice, I thought, and I wondered if maybe she worked in the schoolhouse next door. While she was waiting she reached into her purse, took out a magazine, and started reading the horoscopes. I'd never seen a teacher reading horoscopes in the café, I must have been mistaken. She was just a beautiful young woman for no apparent reason, what was she doing around here? I served her her coffee with a little square of chocolate on the side, and since she seemed to be lost in her beauty and in this bar I went on to ask her, like an idiot, "Will that be all?" She nodded, after a little pause, as if she really had to think about it. I felt like a complete fool, but anyway. I've been so crazy about women in my life. I've known a certain number of them, it's only natural when you're fifty-six years old, in the end I've turned into a fairly well-behaved barman, and when I go home to my place at Quatre-Routes all I have are old memories of the women I've known, and dreams that scare me, most of the time. Time for a breather at last.

"Getting along OK?" I asked Madeleine, beside me.

"Oh yes, just great, no problem."

She gave me a smile like she'd just passed the driver's license exam. No getting around it, though, the boss's wife was going to have to call Sabrina and find out how long before she'd be back. Seeing that she'd turned away to deal with one of the last lunchtime debit cards, Madeleine took the opportunity to ask me very quietly what her problem was, looking so gloomy all the time? I made my dimwit face, like I didn't have the faintest idea, and then, looking at the beautiful woman, I told her it would probably all blow over in the end, just like it always has before. I usually don't deal with clearing the tables. I'm the barman, my business is the bar. Madeleine took care of that, and meantime the boss's wife went back out onto the front step, a gust of wind blew into the dining room, bringing one single dead chestnut leaf with it. It came gliding along and landed about two meters from the bar, some of the customers turned around to watch it. I don't know why that made me feel so sad. Pierrot, you're going soft, brother. There was only one table still full, four gentlemen talking loudly, I recognized the deputy mayor, a dentist, and then I remembered my appointment the day after next in the Social Security medical center in La Garenne. I'd told the boss, but if he was really was discombobulated as he seemed, I was going to have to kiss my extraction goodbye. It didn't hurt anymore with the antibiotics.

I drew myself a beer, strongly discouraged in my condition of course, the young woman was turning her pages, and outside it was getting windier and windier. She didn't seem in any hurry. Pierrot my friend, I told myself. I didn't really tell myself anything at all, as a matter of fact. Really now, don't look at her too much. *Pierrot mon ami* was the name of one of the books that young guy was reading with his cup of coffee and glass of water, last week I think. She was too beautiful for Pierrot, my friend or not. Too young. Too this and too that. Or too not enough.

"How much do I owe you?"

"One euro."

I picked up her ten-euro bill, and she left us a twenty-centime tip, all the same. Le Cercle hasn't raised its price for a cup of coffee, unlike La Rotonde, where they charge one ten. Now there were fewer people heading in and out of the station through the underpass. Before she left, the beautiful woman took a pack of cigarettes from her purse, and since it was a typical woman's purse I had the great pleasure of offering her a light, I always keep a Bic in the pocket of my black vest, along with my matches. There was a touch of green in her eyes, I got a nice look. "Thanks." "Have a good day." "You too." I must have seemed like the classic kindly old barman, as much a part of the scenery as the pretty ladies who come in for a quick cup of coffee while they read their silly magazines, then go on their way, leaving a delicate whiff of jasmine briefly drifting over the bar, which I then began to wipe down. How long would I go on remembering this customer if she didn't come back? I carefully erased my daily slate. Whatever wasn't right. There were probably a few spots left, though. I was doing my best, but you know. One day I'd be able to hang up my mop rag, and then there'd be no place for me here or in any other café of the Hauts-de-Seine area, where I will have spent the greater part of my life, working.

Amédée came out of the kitchen with a cigarette between his lips, he went toward the Casio and sat staring into the distance, smoking a Marlboro, he got them tax-free from his cousins in Brazzaville. He had beautiful little cousins in every country in black Africa. He'd done a lot of traveling before he ended up here in our twelve-square-meter kitchen. He asked for a glass of milk, very white. I'd heard him crack that joke a hundred times before, but it still made me laugh. Nobody but him had the right to make it without getting a good cold stare in return. My pal Amédée.

The boss's wife came over to me. It was after three, and still no word from him. The two of us sat down, Madeleine was getting ready to leave, after her raincoat she put on a fresh coat of lipstick. She said goodbye and headed across the pedestrian street. The boss's wife seemed to have forgotten her already, or maybe not, but she had other things on her mind. The last of the lunch crowd paid with meal tickets. There weren't many customers left. At this point I usually take some time for a break, after the bar work is done I plant myself on a stool and read the news in *Le Parisien* or the local paper. There are the horse races, too, but I never bet anymore. Other people do the same thing, especially in the morning with their coffee, then they usually make a call on their cellphone and go off to deal with their little tasks. I was feeling pretty well worn out, the boss's wife sighed as she looked at me. We sat down facing each other, her on the banquette, me on a chair.

"So, Pierre, how's everything going?"

I didn't know how to answer right off.

"The new girl's getting along well. Any idea when Sabrina'll be back?"

"Sabrina?"

The boss's wife had pretty blue-framed glasses with rhinestones at the corners, they sort of made you think of a Caribbean moth, I'd seen them in the window of the optician's on Maurice-Bokanovski. Oh no, not Sabrina. She came a little closer, and then I was really paying attention, because for more than a few days I'd been wondering if that hadn't occurred to her too. She looked toward the door again, as if he was finally going to come back like the last times he'd ditched us, waiting for five o'clock to come around, when the bar crowds have picked up again. I get off around seven but I'm never a stickler about leaving on time, what have I got to do at home? I'm just a barman, and the longer I stay on the more life goes by in the best possible way. So there we are.

"Pierre, I'm not a child anymore, you know."

I felt like the idiot I was, and I didn't know how to answer. In my business you've always got plenty to do behind the bar, so naturally you don't listen too closely to the words coming at you over the countertop. Most of the time people don't even want you to answer, they only want you to listen, and sometimes it's enough just to be there, without really paying attention. Most of all, I take care never to keep them waiting, to let them pay their bill when they're ready to go, or else leave them in peace the whole time they're here.

"I know, ma'am, I know that very well."

I gave her a smile, but I still wonder what my face must have looked like just then. Of course she knew, she just wanted to hear me say it. Fortunately Amédée started yelling about something in the kitchen, and then he came out in his beautiful pearl-gray suit, with his black wool scarf and his walkman, his day was done. He gave us a nod. "See you tomorrow, Amédée."

"Ma'am, we've got to get the dishwasher fixed, I'm not a plumber, for Christ's sake! It's leaking! Jesus, I've had it with this dump!"

It was two weeks since our last flood, and then – I'd figured this out while I was washing the glasses, a little while before – it was last spring that the boss started to seem so out of sorts, with their daughter abroad and Sabrina right in front of him from morning to night. He was forty-three, it's like a sickness sometimes, those things.

"I really can't imagine where he might be," I told the boss's wife.

I felt like a good stiff drink, here I am fifty-six years old and often I think I can feel the kid in me coming back to the surface, or is that just my imagination again?

"Pierre, you know very well where he is."

This time I wasn't going to get off that easy, and in any case it made me sad to see her so miserable. Like I say, the boss isn't such a bad guy, but she was a real peach of a woman, most of the time.

"This is making me uncomfortable, boss. You don't know when Sabrina's coming back?"

We stopped talking at that point.


Outside the sky was clearing after the morning's gray clouds and wind, or at least that's how it looked from the bar. I'm a weather nut, I don't really know why. Bars can help us in fair weather and foul, for me it doesn't make that much difference, except on my way home at night or on my day off. The boss's wife stood up before I could, it was the young man in black, this place was getting to be a habit for him. He still had the same face, still a little like a child, slightly anemic by the look of him, she asked what he wanted and I heard the coffee machine going. I wanted to get up and head back to work, but it was clear there was no ducking out of it this time. Pierrot my friend. We'd see about that. When she came back she started stacking the ashtrays to go empty them out, and I told her I was just about to do that, if she didn't mind waiting we could talk if she liked. She looked at me like I'd made a stupid joke, then took a Kleenex from her purse, she had tears in her eyes. That hit me in the pit of my stomach, not that I was worried what people might think, the young man was taking this all in via the big mirror behind the bottles, where my raincoat was hanging. I keep my wallet and keys behind the cash register, you never know.

"Ma'am, look at me."

I took her by the shoulders like an old lover in a movie on Channel 3, the kind they put on too late. The next day, if I didn't watch it all the way to the end, I keep it going while I'm at work. I've seen stars sit down at my bar, especially back when I was working in Paris. She looked up at me, and then she did an amazing thing, I'd never seen the like in all my time at this job, and I've been at it since I was nineteen. I don't even want to count how many years I've been in the bar business, not including those six months on disability after the end of my last love affair, I was fifty-three when I came back. She nestled between my arms. "Pierre, oh Pierre, if you only knew." What a dope he was, I thought. All this for Sabrina, and then I wanted to tell her everything would work out in the end, she just had to give him some time, and also I'd been thinking it might be good for them to get away for a while together, except that you can't close a bar like Le Cercle, even for a week in October, without the next week's take falling off by a good forty percent. And then how do you pay Amédée, and the waitress on sick leave, and her replacement, and the old barman who just wants to be left alone and keep listening to his customers tell their stories without once asking him what he thinks? She even let out a few real sobs, carefully stifled, and I felt like squeezing her tight to make them stop.

"Ma'am," I murmured, "you've got to get hold of yourself, people are looking."

The youngster wasn't missing a second of the show. He did have a book to read, after all, right beside him. She raised her head, she wanted to tell me something, but suddenly she pushed me away and ran to the door at the far end of the bar, she went up to their apartment. I haven't been there often, after all the years I'd put in here I knew quite enough about them as it was. I'd never tried to spend much time with them. For two summers, while they were away and I wasn't, I'd gone up to water their plants and sort through their mail, and that was it. This thing with the boss's wife had really shaken me up, and that's no lie.

I'm only a barman, and when I forget that, the world around me seems like a bunch of different movies running at the same time. There are romance movies and sad movies, and if you pay attention most of their stories start to get all mixed together, till there's no way you can go on telling them to yourself. It's like they're all chasing after each other, and then, just when you're ready to decide how they end, you have to serve two beers and wipe down the counter again, and empty the ashtrays and scrub out the coffee machine, and now and then leave the bar with butterflies in your stomach to go hear the results of a blood test or chest x-ray, and then it's to hell with the film, and good riddance. It came back to me a little while later, I was alone, the evening's first customers were drifting in. Everything was lit up around the underpass. They don't do things by half-measures here in Asnières. The boss gripes on and on about the way our local taxes keep going up (and the government health and pension contributions, and insurance, and Social Security, and the business tax, and the residence tax), but at least we have Christmas wreaths starting in mid-October, for the big sales period. It doesn't do all that much to cheer things up around here, but people like it. The customers were keeping me busy again. I'd got the message, she wanted me to go have a talk with the boss. I shrugged my shoulders a few times without meaning to, and when the kid in black asked how much he owed me I said it was on the house, in honor of the boss's wife. He didn't know how to answer, he already had the money in his hand, and now he put it back in his pocket. He must have been waiting for his chance to get going, for me it's just a pleasure to have a little chat. I worked like a madman for another two hours. Usually I had the boss there to help with the customers, in theory at least, but now I was all alone. I didn't answer when the regulars asked questions, I said "They'll be back, nothing to worry about, what'll it be?" I hardly spoke a word to Roger, who's been my friend for thirty years now. He'd told me he'd be coming by so we could make plans for the weekend, we have a little betting system we like to try out together, this time we were thinking of Longchamp.

"You're swamped, huh?" he asked me.

"Worse than that."

He was wearing a nice blue shirt, and for the past few weeks he'd been going jogging by the river every few days. He'd tried to get me to come with him. Fat chance! His new girl was thirty-seven. I didn't notice when he got up to leave, I haven't seen him in such a hurry for five years at least.

"So we'll call each other?"

"Yeah, be seeing you, sorry!"

It was already dark at eight, when I got a chance for a breather. I was completely done in. Usually I'm back home in Les Grésillons by this time.

There was a young couple camped out at a table in back. I went over and started to clean up all around them, but they kept right on making out. They were getting on my nerves, the boss's wife still hadn't come down. I told the holdouts that closing time had come. In England they have a bell, when it rings the people leave without making a fuss, as orderly as you please. The boss's daughter says there are always taxis waiting just for the drunks, with a special rate. That place must be a boozer's paradise. Oh, Pierrot, am I tired. This was a fine establishment before the boss started chasing after his life. The young couple finally left, they seemed very much in love, the way people are when it's part-time, if you don't mind my saying. This evening they'll be texting each other in secret. Who was I to think that? I had the keys to Le Cercle, fortunately I'd kept them on me, because of everything that had happened these past few weeks, I suppose. I decided to leave her in peace. I turned off the lights, then the Casio, now things had quieted down out in the street. The newsstand was already closed, and the Relais H too, the people coming through the underpass were all in a hurry. Often you'll seem them carrying a baguette at this time of night, because they're not sure there'll be any left in the bakery. Some of them walk quicker in the morning than in the evening, with others it's the reverse. Apart from that, nothing much going on. I've never been to my bosses' place when they were around, except once when Sophie was heading off to England, and then another time when the boss had been at it again and was having one of his crises. I sat on a stool and looked toward the station, no one there but the young guys holding up the wall by the photo shop. I thought of Sabrina. If he was at her place he'd be back soon for sure, because if I knew her she'd never let him stay with her two kids around, Jacques and Élise, although in private she called them Jasmine and Hamid, that's the boy. Sometimes she showed me their pictures, she took a lot. I'd also seen her kids a few times when she was picking them up after a weekend at their father's. Now and then they went to the movies at the Alcazar, next door. Last year I'd taken the little boy to one of the Levallois team's basketball games. A colleague in the business there got me a good deal on the tickets. Lord, I realized, I was exhausted. I called the boss's wife from the bar. She waited almost a quarter of a ring before she picked up, without speaking a word.

"It's Pierre, I've closed up."

"Pierre? Oh yes, Pierre. Thanks."

She was sobbing like nobody's business, and I'm not made of stone, I told myself they really were lucky to have found someone like me, by tomorrow I would have forgotten this whole thing, honestly.

"Listen, do you want me to come up?"

"If you like, Pierre. No, I'll come down."

So I hung up too, and then while I was waiting I went and put on a little cashmere sweater my most recent girlfriend gave me, it's gotten all pilly now, but it's light and it keeps you warm. I combed my hair and washed my hands, and then, in the mirror, maybe because the lighting was dim, I told myself I hadn't done too badly, even on a day like this.

I put on my raincoat and looked out toward the sycamores. The branches were lit up by the lights over the tracks. They were swollen-looking and milky white, just like in the dream I'd been having for the past several nights. I hadn't yet told Roger about it to see what he thought. I'm a superstitious guy, especially now that I live alone. It's just that I have too much time to myself, really. With no one there to answer me, I come up with some very odd ideas sometimes. Or often I talk to my mother, who isn't around anymore either. I call Roger to talk about this and that. But that's not enough for me. Some days I'd rather not have to come out from behind my bar at all, but there's no getting around it, life is still on the other side. I smoked a cigarette while I was waiting for her. My fourth of the day, that was something at least. When she came down I turned toward the stairway door, she'd made herself up and put on her leather jacket, and she'd taken off her glasses. I thought she looked pretty as a picture, but this was no time for compliments.

"I haven't done the cash register," I told her.

She looked at me like I was speaking Medieval Chinese, and then when she understood she gave me a nod.

"Would you like something to drink?"

She said "What's that, Pierre? What on earth are you talking about?"

I answered, "Nothing, nothing," and she sat down on a stool at one end of the bar, all dressed up to go out. The young man in black liked to park himself on that same stool. There was also that beautiful woman this morning, and in one corner of my mind I wondered if she might be coming to see me tonight behind my eyelids, with her delicious perfume. They haven't invented Viagra for dreams yet. That might come in handy sometimes.

"I don't know what to do, Pierre, he's slipping away from me."

She opened her purse, she had two full packs of cigarettes. I tried to find something to say, but like any barman I'm much better with my ears, and then the good thing about your ears is you can decide what to hear.

"Pierre, do you think he's in love with her?"

She said that in a very low voice, very gentle, whereas as a boss she makes a habit of not mincing words, and especially of saying them very loudly, particularly when she's talking to Amédée in his kitchen, or to the guy who comes to wash dishes, one of the old temps from the trade school. That question really rattled me, and I had to sit down on the stool next to hers so it wouldn't show. Pierrot my friend, now's the time to keep your trap shut. "Yes, ma'am," I heard myself answer. And at that point I would have happily bit my tongue, but there was no taking it back now, so there we were.

"You should call Sabrina. Why don't you call her?"

She looked at the ceiling, they'd had it redone just two years before, but what with all the cigarettes and all the life coming and going in this café, it wasn't as clean as it used to be. La Rotonde was closing down too, now. Sometimes the new owners stay open late, on Fridays they have karaoke, and they also show soccer games on the big screen. The boss went back and forth on that for a long time, and finally he went for the renovation, we could see about soccer later. She sighed very loudly, then said "No, I'm not going to call her." All of a sudden she turned toward me with a little smile far sweeter than any I'd seen for the past five or six years of my life.

"Incidentally, I was wondering, how long have you been working here?"

"Ever since Longardi's time, you remember? It must be eight years now."

"Yes, that's right, eight years. Sophie was in seventh grade when we came here."

We were really alone in the café, her and I.

I loved those days, back when the kid was going to school in the neighborhood, she used to do her homework at a table in the back of the dining room. Sometimes she even wanted me to help with her poetry recitations, and I'd play the fox or the crow or the turkey or the lion-king from La Fontaine's fables. I'd never studied poetry much before I came to work here. She giggled like crazy. She got good grades and extra points for good behavior, when she got ten of those they gave her a set of little pictures as a reward. The boss's wife went on smiling at those memories a little while longer, and then she looked at the people coming out of the tunnel. Whenever he wasn't among them she must have been telling herself he'd be on the next train, in seven minutes if he was coming from Saint-Lazare, eleven if it was the other way. I had nothing to add, because of my advanced age, and as for what family I have, I haven't seen them for some time now, I've never been comfortable with all that.

"At least *you're* faithful."

"Thank you, ma'am."

She sighed again, to snap herself out of it. I saw a guy squinting and waving his arms at us. He'd just come out of La Rotonde and didn't feel like going home yet. I gestured no with one hand, and he set off for the next café, talking very loudly and waving his arms again, he was very put out.

"What do you think of the new girl?"

I looked at the boss's wife and said what I thought, that she was very good. Yes, very good.

"She lives a bit far away, though. Don't you think she'd be better off finding a job closer to home?"

I put on the standard face of the guy who has nothing to say, I don't want to cause problems for anyone, in my work as a barman. She stood up, went to the cash register, and took out two bills. "Pierre, I'd like to invite you to dinner, OK?" I almost swallowed my barman's bowtie, but it was back in my dresser drawer, so no harm done. I told her sure, if she liked, I'd be happy to, it was on me. She said no, on her. She held out the keys to her little black Audi, which I would have found very tempting in the old days, back when I lived in Paris myself, near the Gare du Nord. I always lived close to one of the big train stations when I was in Paris. I'm not sure that was deliberate. We left the café together after giving the dining room one last check. She went into the kitchen, and when she came out she was walking more like her usual self. And it wasn't just her walk, either. Women in cafés all walk the same way, judging by my long experience of these things, it's certainly no job for foot-draggers. We set off toward her car.

She turned back toward Le Cercle's front window, the lights were all off. There was only a little red glow over the awning of their apartment's front door, that was the alarm system. And then, in the café window, the ads for the different beers, Pelforth at the moment, posters for exhibitions in the community center, the schedule for La Lanterne, which is a neighborhood movie theater over by the Levallois bridge, the kind you almost never see anywhere else. The only one I could compare it to is the Jean-Vigo, in the old Cité-Jardin development in Gennevilliers, but who goes to see movies in places like that anymore?

"You OK?"

She didn't answer.

"Don't worry, Pierre."

There were dead leaves on the windshield, stuck down by the rain. I picked them off one by one, and I didn't tell the boss's wife they were scattered all over the floor of Le Cercle in my past few nights' dream. I opened her door, as if I were also a chauffeur in my off hours, and her a princess every now and again.

"Fall's come for good now," she told me in a quiet voice.

"Yes, that's very true."

What I really wanted to say I kept to myself, she wasn't listening anyway. I walked around the car and wondered where she might like to eat. Could it be she'd decided to go to Sabrina's herself? Try to patch things up with him, if that was still possible? I had no idea. We ended up on the Place Voltaire. Her little Audi was a pleasure to drive. First I drove along the quais, for the past few days it had rained more or less regularly, not that much, but still, the Seine was churning. The river always shines a little under the streetlamps on the banks, and a little more when the wind is blowing against the current.

"Where do you want to go, Pierre?"

I almost told her I wanted to go home and let them sort out their marital problems for themselves, but it was too late, I thought, I'm already fifty-six. I drove back through the little streets on the other side of the station, in the nice part of Asnières where you find the villas and the model apartments overlooking the river, set a little ways back from the street. And so we went by Le Cercle again, I went straight ahead down the Avenue de la Marne toward Les Bourguignons. There was still some traffic, she was looking out the window, sometimes she opened her mouth and murmured things I didn't understand. I was used to that. Around here the bars were still open, they're too far away to give us much competition, especially the ones over by Les Grésillons. People there don't have much money to spend.

I know this neighborhood like the back of my hand. If it had been up to me I would gladly have driven around for another hour or two, going nowhere in particular, but that wouldn't have done much to pick up her spirits, and that's what she needed, I thought. She gave me a strange look when I parked on the Place Voltaire, I said "I was thinking of couscous, how does that sound?" "OK, Pierre, yes, now that you mention it, couscous. Why not?" We went into the brasserie, a regular haunt of mine since I became a confirmed bachelor, and I was very grateful that the waitress didn't make any cracks. She just gave a little giggle, out of the corner of her eye. I took that as a compliment. We ordered a couscous for two, the boss's wife didn't know what she wanted, we settled on a *complet*: lamb, chicken, merguez. We had a kir on the house, courtesy of Gérard the Kabyle, whose real name is Slimane. I asked the boss's wife what she was planning to do, in the end? She picked at her food all through the meal. She had no idea. She was going to wait, Pierrot, what else could she do? This was all starting to get me down, especially with such a nice couscous in front of me. Myself, I'm over all that love business, really. She did finally start to tell me some things, though, and while she was talking I saw two or three guys I knew, just regular decent guys in their way, more or less like me, they left us alone. They'd met, she was eighteen and him twenty, she'd dropped her nursing studies to follow him.

"We were head over heels in love, Pierrot, do you know how that is?"

"Um . . . I've been there, ma'am, yes, I think."

But she wasn't really expecting an answer. I didn't want to let her down, she could spill it all out for me, and then, not too late I hoped, I could go home to bed. He was something of a maverick in those days, and he'd never gone to college. They started out doing seasonal work on the Côte d'Azur, and her parents refused to see her anymore, because of him.

"Because of him, ma'am?"

"Yes, for three years."

She smiled at me.

It surprised me to think of them in love that way, and then I realized he must be having one hell of a mid-life crisis to walk out on a love like that. And then after their daughter Sophie they never had another kid. She would have liked at least one son, but all he could think of was work, that and the races, where he lost lots of money. "You know how he is." He was always wanting to move on, some guys are like that, they just know life would be better or more beautiful if they could only go somewhere else.

I heard her out to the end, but on the whole I don't think there was anything I didn't already know. It just made me a little uncomfortable, because from now on it was going to be awkward working for them, I'm not paid to be a third wheel, if you don't mind my saying.

"Do you think Sabrina's pretty?"

"Yes, of course" was the only answer to that one. There was no saying the opposite, particularly because I knew she was all alone in the world, with her family she never saw anymore, back in the new North Amiens suburbs, and two children to look after. She never said a word against her ex-husband, but I'd seen enough of him in the bar to get an idea. The rest of the meal went by in silence. She got out her cigarettes, and I smoked another one.

Little by little I was losing the habit, but I still liked to smoke. The waitress came to ask how everything was, and I made the classic no-complaints gesture as a way of avoiding the dessert menu, which wasn't worth much in that place. But they do serve a real mint tea, with pine nuts.

"What do you say? Would you like a cup?"

She was looking outside toward the square, now a mist was falling. There was a police van parked by the hammam, the city's planning to tear down half the block from here to the Gennevilliers métro stop. I've heard lots of people around here don't have their papers in order. They're always changing apartments, they pass them along hand to hand, and often those hands are holding plastic bags from the cheap Tati stores. Where will the people go then? That's the kind of question I ask myself nowadays. I investigate little nothings like that, it keeps me occupied. For several years now I've been wanting to start taking photos again, but I don't do it often. I also stopped collecting postcards after my last separation. Why? Is it because I live alone that I feel like looking into that sort of thing? Or maybe because I'm getting old? The waitress brought us our tea, along with an assortment of little cakes, I'd have to thank the Kabyle. He was away that night, one of his young cousins had a bantamweight boxing match, a regular from the Aubervilliers ring, where everybody has a broken nose at least, and the cops come once a month. They know me around here, I told myself, no question about that.

"Here we are, ma'am, help yourself."

She smiled at me, me or the cakes. I could see so many memories shining in her eyes, just on the brink of tears. I know that feeling myself, but I've forgotten it, mostly. Yes, I forgot all that long ago, but I still have my regrets, in the evening, when I come home from work and have nothing to keep me busy. It was ten-thirty by the time we were done. I had to excuse myself to go to the bathroom. I saw her taking out her cellphone as I opened the door in back, she'd been doing that a lot since he disappeared. When I was done I found her waiting outside. She wanted to make sure I wouldn't be paying for dinner.

There was a guy on the sidewalk down the street from the métro, I saw him every night, he must have been an Arab too. He was walking his dog, smoking a cigarette. Often you'd see him making wild threatening gestures at the people going by, but then when you came up beside him he always said good evening. Roger knew him better than me, they were neighbors back when he lived by the Social Security offices at Quatre-Routes.

He'd noticed him getting stranger and stranger, and then one day he didn't come home. He had a problem with the moon, my pal says. Some sort of score to settle with it. Why not, after all? He started up again as soon as you walked away. It was surprising at first, but not to his dog, who could clearly care less. It stood there the whole time, staring into the appliance store, the Moroccan cyber-café where they sell phone cards for calling abroad, and the bazaar with its pots and pans and bric-à-brac and socks two euros for six pairs, and underwear too, fuchsia and turquoise, and those white Petit-Bateau numbers for the kids, all stacked up in piles. And above all that, there wasn't a star to be seen.

"You're cold, aren't you?"

I thought I saw her shivering a little, but no, it really wasn't cold. She looked at me when the guy turned down the little street toward the ruined houses and stone-broke families. It's not a good neighborhood, down that way. I didn't live around there, but I went by it every day. You can get attached to those things too, you can also get attached to people you don't even know, you're alone . . .

"He's turned off his cellphone, what the hell is he doing?"

The mist was fogging up her glasses.

"Well, shall I take you home, Pierre? I'll drop you off, and then I'm going to head home myself."

I took her arm as we crossed the street, we weren't in the walk. I tried to find something to say when we pulled up to my building, but I was out of ideas. "See you tomorrow, then?" I got out of the car and bent down beside her, she was taking out her cellphone again. "All right, have a safe trip home." She nodded, then looked my way.

"I just have to wait for him, Pierre, he'll come back in the end."

"Yes, of course he will. See you tomorrow."

I shut the car door gently and watched her speed off down my street. I climbed up to the fourth floor, we have a wooden staircase in my building. I don't pay much rent, but we have a wooden staircase all the same. I hear it was built in the thirties. The last time I was part of a couple I lived in a new building, a one-bedroom apartment with all the amenities, and a built-in kitchen. We even had underground parking. But I never felt at home there. The woman's name was Jacqueline Serradura, and for her it was a kind of triumph to be renting an apartment like that, we had all sorts of differences of that type. Still, we tried, her especially, I think. I just turned out not to be right for her.

Or maybe our time was already up, and we just didn't know it? And there were a bunch of other stupid little things that came between us. We had trouble understanding each other, we really should have tried harder. But as time went by those differences got to me, till I just couldn't take them anymore. I tried, though. At least I think I did. And then after that, as a way of forgetting it all, I got sick.

# II

In this building things are better. There's that squeaking stair-case to remind me of my childhood, and also we all know each other a little. We have a few ordinary couples living quiet lives, and there are also two families with very young children, and on the top floor some students from Mali and poor folks of various nationalities, as well as a student who must be in her thirties and gets a lot of afternoon callers, if you don't mind my saying. For the past year she's been wearing a single red lock in the middle of her hair. I always want to pull it whenever I see her. I make her laugh by asking how much she'd charge me just for that? One time she wasn't in a laughing mood, she explained that all the men who came to her room asked her that very same question. "Is that right?" Yes, or at least they wanted to, even if they didn't ask. It was even worse when she was a little girl and her mother made her wear pigtails. There's a lesson in that. I would never have imagined such a thing, to tell the truth. Sometimes she comes by my place to ask for some salt or borrow a cigarette, or just to have a little chat.

"I'm not disturbing you, Pierrounet?"

"Not at all. On the contrary. You're well?"

"I won't stay long."

I don't even know her real first name, the mailbox only has her family name. She calls herself Jessica. She told me she'd had so many different first names these last few years that she'd ended up forgetting her own. What would she do if she wound up with a psycho on her hands? I'd immediately regretted that question, because a minute after I'd asked it she went on her way. I like hearing her talk. And then the things she tells me make a change from Le Cercle. I gave her a copy of my keys one day when they were coming to read the meters. I've never been up to the sixth floor, I suppose that must be why. We all get on well together, it seems to me. The old woman on the second floor's mind is starting to go, but when she leaves her keys in the lock someone always watches for her and lets her back into the building. I do her shopping on Sundays, she gives me chocolates at Christmas, and on her good days I take her to the market, arm in arm. I lost my mother when I was 42, she was my adoptive mother, that was far too young for my liking, and it still is today.

It was a quarter past twelve, and it wasn't going to be a long night, assuming I took two or three urgent measures to ward off insomnia. Was it because I'd had dinner out that I found myself in such an inexplicably fine mood? Because I hadn't been alone tonight, like I was every other night? Or maybe because the boss's wife had taken me aside? He really should have come home earlier, or else he should have left long ago, if that's what he wanted to do. Or so it seems to me, at my age, though I'm not really all that sure. When I was thirty I went out for a pack of cigarettes, as they say, except in this case it was true. I smoked Craven A's, as I recall. All the tobacconists are closed Sundays here in the suburbs, of course. It took me a while to get my hands on a pack, and then I made my decision just as I was opening it, I remember it well. I smoked a bunch of cigarettes one after another, I couldn't stop myself. I didn't go home either. Was I really unhappy with her, or had I just stopped believing in us, in all that? I can't even remember. I only remember the pack of Craven A's. That's what my mother smoked too, I think. I signed the divorce papers on the corner of a bar, where I also poured myself a good number of drinks, for me, at the time. It was probably for the best. At that age the thought of children never entered my mind, the fatherhood routine didn't interest me at all. And then afterwards it was too late. It took me a few years to really regret that, and since then I've never stopped asking myself questions. Was I right? Would I have left her if I hadn't run out of smokes? I always keep my apartment neat and tidy. It must be living alone that's made me so fussy, but it suits me like that, with everything in its place. Sometimes when I come home after work I feel completely alone, but not tonight, with my head full of my employers' troubles, and then all those other people too, I never see them for very long in the course of a day, but when all's said and done, even if we're not exactly acquainted, we're never really apart. They keep me company when they're not around. Meantime, the boss's wife was one hell of a woman. I sat down on my couch, it's true that she'd cracked a little tonight before we went to the Kabyle's place, but all day long she'd managed Le Cercle like nothing had happened. If he wasn't at Sabrina's, where was he? If he weren't my boss I would have gone and told him there was no room for a guy like him in her life, with her two children to raise. The fact is, his time was already past. He probably couldn't take getting old either.

I realized I hadn't turned on the TV set I was staring at, and I wanted to see the late news on Channel 3. Eventually you get tired of the news around Asnières, which isn't really news at all, actually. You don't pay it much mind, apart from the people who've died, and then, because of my work, the changing signs on the storefronts, that Pimkie used to be an Étam, that sort of thing. Even a guy like me needs something more than that. I pushed the button on the remote and immediately turned down the sound so I wouldn't have to hear words I hadn't asked for, I get more than enough of that at work. I saw a fresh-breathed couple kissing behind a waterfall, Rexona deodorant. I'd missed the news. I decided to take a shower, and then I wanted to do my laundry, too. There was one question I couldn't get out of my mind: what would happen if he didn't come back? I couldn't even imagine that, of course. He'd celebrated his forty-third birth-day just before they left on vacation, all the regulars were there, they'd chipped in for a present. It's strange, too, I would never have seen the boss's wife as a nurse.

When I was out sick at Beaujon Hospital two years ago I ended up in the more-or-less attentive hands of a beautiful fat Carib-bean girl, a little Franco-Moroccan homo, and a Spanish woman who danced the salsa every Friday night in an Argentinian restau-rant near the Gare de l'Est. She used to practice her moves while she was getting my morning pills together. Salsa was really the only thing she cared about. She wasn't afraid of sick people, and I never got the feeling I put her off. It was watching her dance the salsa at Beaujon that brought me back to life. Before I was dis-charged she even found me a place to take lessons in Paris, I went two or three times. I didn't have much talent, but I would have been happy to keep at it if I had a regular partner. I thanked her with one of my favorite postcards, which shows a kid running down the middle of the street with a baguette. I never dared to go back to the cardiology ward and pay her a visit. What would she have thought? I liked that girl. It was half past midnight. I took a quick little shower, fairly cold, waiting for things to calm down in my head, but this time it didn't work. It really was no ordinary day. I put on my bathrobe and looked up the boss's cellphone number in the address book I keep by the phone. He must have thought it was her, I got the answering machine. I said I would have liked to talk to him, we all needed to know what the hell was going on, and then soon there'd be the orders to send in to the wholesaler in Gennevilliers and the Rungis market. That was his responsibility. I was about to say goodnight when all of a sudden he picked up, like he'd been there all along, waiting to pounce, if you'll pardon the expression.

"Ah, Pierre, it's you, hi, how'd it go today?"

"It went fine, yes, just fine. Monsieur Dilman paid up, by the way."

I could picture the look on his face, preoccupied and not very interested, and then, because it was getting late, I added:

"You really should tell us when you're planning to come back. You've got to call your wife."

I Ie didn't answer. I heard him swallow, with my one ear I tried to make out where he might be, but there wasn't a sound. Maybe he was alone, in the end.

"Hey, boss, did you hear me?"

"Yes, yes."

He mulled that over a while, then finally told me he just didn't know for the moment, maybe soon, he'd see, but in any case, if he was away longer than expected, he was counting on me to keep him posted. That was what really jumped out at me: keep him posted. Pierrot my friend, I don't know why those words came into my head, we still weren't out of the woods. Keep you posted on what, my fine fellow, I wondered? On what she thinks of you?

"You can count on me, but you've really got to call your wife, she's worried, you know."

At this point I sensed I was annoying him something fierce, I heard a dog barking, drowning out his anger. It was the bulldog over at number 33c, it really knew how to pick its moment. That dog was a nuisance, there'd already been complaints, a guy at number 31, dumb as a plank, and a family at number 27 who had real twin girls and a Siamese cat.

"Pierre, that's none of your business."

"Well . . . whatever you say, boss, and good evening to you."

It made me mad that he'd taken it so badly. And then, since I always like to follow through on an idea, when I have one, I went to the window and looked down into the street. I opened it and gave him a wave with one hand. I'm sure he saw me. His blinkers were on. He was leaning on the hood, double parked just down-stairs from my place. Today I tell myself I could have run after him and convinced him to come up, he would have talked to me just like a customer in the bar, sort of cleaning house in his head, but what would that have changed? He was just totally lost, if you ask me. I knew next to nothing about his life, only his disap-pearances and his little crises, and the big dents the horses put in the cash register, and then the way he fiddled with his income statements, like any other owner of a café or restaurant. He was just my boss, and that was all.

He turned down the street toward the expressway, and then at the corner he very slowly ran a red light, like the basket case he was at that point. I lit one last cigarette, then poured some detergent into my little basin and set my things to soak. These days I'd rather do my own washing than go to a laundromat. I always think people are wondering what a guy like me's doing in a laundromat, and that bugs me, it's stupid, I know. I'm more than old enough to own my own washing machine. Before he found himself a girlfriend, Roger and I used to go together, like old bachelors. I brought the fabric softener, and the time went by faster with the two of us watching the clock together, telling each other our stories. Now he gives his laundry to Muriel. But still. I also took my two antibiotic pills. The pain was back when I woke up from last night's dream, and I couldn't afford two bad nights in a row, not after a day like today. Deep down I'm a relaxed kind of guy, like most of my colleagues in the business, from what I've seen. But I'm also a worn-out kind of guy, as it happens. After that I smeared Nivea on my face like I do every night, on the off chance it might do something for me, you never know.

Sometimes when I go to bed I read a page or two of a book and don't even have time to realize I haven't understood a word. Other nights I can read a good ten pages or so, which is no small feat for a little guy like me. That night I was reading *If This Is a Man*, because back in September that's what the youngster who comes to Le Cercle with his black clothes and his cellphone was reading, and his eyes were shining the whole time. And then, you've got to keep up on things. In that respect my profession's not particularly challenging. There are the horse races, of course, and car wrecks and crimes, and drunk talk, and sex talk, and customers who get caught by the radar on the riverside roads or coming off the Asnières bridge, and then the occasional troubles at closing time, but apart from that we don't have too much to ponder.

*If This Is a Man* is the story of a Jewish Italian resistance fighter who lived through the concentration camps, he wanted to bear witness. He worked as a chemist to keep body and soul together. I'd asked the young man the author's name, and he seemed very excited to give it to me, he even wrote it down on the cardboard coaster I'd handed him, I've still got it in my apartment. He was some guy, that Monsieur Primo Levi. There's somebody I would have loved to have as a customer. It stirred me up to see the kid in such a state. I read twenty-one pages. I would even have kept going if I hadn't had to go back to Le Cercle early to keep an eye on developments. Le Cercle was closed, and no one had thought to unlock the door for me. My friend Pierrot, lost in a bad dream. Inside I could see more and more dead leaves all over the big gray and white floor tiles. I knocked on the glass door and fumbled with the key, but all around it seemed like people were avoiding me. I thought I saw Sabrina and her two kids, but when I came closer to ask what was happening she got scared and started to run, her two children were pulling at her to make her hurry up. There was no sound in my dream, even though I ended up yelling like crazy. And that was that. I woke up at six in the morning covered in sweat, I went to drink a glass of water and pee. I picked up Primo Levi's book again, I was hoping to sleep a little longer, but nothing doing. Pierrot, you've got to get up. I was sick of that stupid dream, and especially of waking up afterwards. Would I never know how it ended, assuming it did?

Still, that night went by better than the one before. It made me happy to be among the first ones up in my building. The street was lit up by the three lights under my windows. Sometimes I hope for another beautiful day as I'm opening my shutters, I can feel it taking shape inside me, and I'm not talking about the weather. I get up at six, which leaves me more than an hour to myself before I set off for work, and I try to make the most of it.

It started to rain when I left my building at seven. I looked into Le Voltigeur on the Rue Alibert to see if my pal Roger was there, but no, only his boss, who'd just cranked up the metal shutter. We waved hello. Then I picked up the pace, because even with my umbrella I could feel my pantcuffs getting wet. I like walking in the morning, but this time I heard the 161 bus coming up behind me, and since I was almost at the Mathurins stop I raised my hand to get on. There was already quite a crowd. The office workers get off at the station to take their train, the others go on to the warehouses and the last few factories a little further along, we're all together, just a little tired. That beast's easier to spot in the morning than at night. Sometimes it seems like it's been with us since the day of our birth, here in the 161 bus. And then no, after all, you catch a glance, a face, and things are much better than you think.

I sat down in the very front of the bus, I looked out the window, I can't even say I saw much, my reflection maybe, but that film's the same every time. I was going to be very early for work. That's what I'd decided to do, just in case he wasn't there and she hadn't come down. In my mind he'd be coming back in the evening, after calling to let us know. I also thought about my mother, two stops before mine. Sometimes I could go for days without thinking of her. Other times, in spite of my fifty-six years, she showed up day after day, at all hours, to tell me "Work hard in school," "Don't forget to buy bread," "Don't touch yourself like that Pierrot, you'll make yourself sick," she'd never stopped watching over me, especially now that I live alone.

"Where are you going, Pierrot?"

I think I must have smiled like an idiot, because this time she was coming to visit me early in the morning. I told her "Don't worry, mama, I'm just going to work," but then I put a quick stop to that because I'd made eye contact with a woman I often saw early in the morning at Le Cercle. I'd talk to her later, I told myself. I gave the woman a nod, luckily she hadn't heard anything. We take the same bus almost every morning, but we've never talked. She always used to order a cup of coffee with a little eye-opener on the side, but a few months earlier she'd got a new hairstyle, cut short and dyed blonde, and she'd given up on the calvados. I'd never seen her there with a guy, maybe there wasn't one? I liked her better before, even if she seemed a little more worn. I thought she looked pretty good this way, but in my head she was still the woman who drank a couple of calvas before lighting her first cigarette of the day and heading off to the Asnières station for her train. She's one of the people I know, just because of my job. Without really meaning to be, we're kind of alike. But we keep to ourselves, we say hello and goodbye, and that's it. Why not, in the end?

I got off with the last few people at the stop by the station, Le Cercle was still locked up tight. There was a light on in their apartment. I'd open the place this morning, and then, a little later, the boss would come down with his sour face on, looking like an overweight Buddha, and everything would go back to normal. What would become of Sabrina? She was backed up against the wall in her wobbly high heels, with a kid under each arm. I cranked up the shutter and turned the key in the lock by the floor, the rain was really coming down now, I had to close my umbrella. I took off my raincoat as soon as I got inside, once I'd started up the Lavazzo and turned on the lights at the box in the kitchen. I kept my sweater on, it still wasn't warm enough for that. I was glad to be alone, I didn't feel like talking. When the boss opened he was always a little chattier than usual till eight in the morning, after that he pretty much kept his mouth shut, apart from the standard how-are-you-how-are-yous with the customers or phone calls from his pals. I gave the bar a good wipe with the mop rag. It didn't really need it, but that was something I liked doing, so why not indulge? You really are a useful thing in other people's lives when you're a barman. The customers don't realize it outright, of course, but when all's said and done, in good times and bad, there's always a bar in their lives, and a barman, a bit wizened but very professional, to serve them whatever they want, and then when they're done they snap out of their little reverie, unless they've been thinking of nothing at all, and when it comes time to go the barman has told them thank you, goodbye, and have a good day. You're rambling, Pierrot. I ran out to get the croissants and baguettes for breakfast. The bakery's right on the corner. The last baker died of the same illness I had three years ago, or so I've heard. I didn't stand around twiddling my thumbs for long. Right away I served three separate coffees, one of them an espresso with extra water, and another with a dash of milk, plus one full breakfast with tea.

An hour later everything was back to normal for me, although I really wished he was here, because I hadn't had time to fix myself a proper breakfast. Things got a lot slower at nine, some low clouds moved in and put a stop to the drizzle, and then when it started up again you could see the rain falling diagonally over the tracks, it was settling in for the day. I was right to put on my sweater, the seasons were changing for sure. I hadn't had time to go look at the Seine, which has been one of my pleasures in life since I came back to the fold of my neighborhood, fifteen years ago. I'd find a moment for that on Sunday, or maybe some other day, I didn't know.

"Don't get too close to the edge, Pierrot!"

"Yes, ma, I know. Bye!"

Usually the boss was heading back up to his apartment by this time, he'd been doing that for years, and then a little later he'd come down with his wife and I'd make her a cup of tea, but not today, it would seem. Amédée came in with a stack of books under one arm, and a bunch of other stuff in a big plastic Leclerc bag. He set his load down on the bar and gave me a big smile. "So how are things, Pierrot? Sleep well?" He was waiting for me to say I was as happy as the Banania man in the old poster he had on his wall, or some other joke like that, but all at once he changed his tune.

"Shit, he's not here? What the fuck's he up to?"

I shook my head no, and he came back behind the bar without asking permission. I didn't make a fuss about it, though, because if we were going to be facing another day with no boss it was best he not be in too bad a mood.

"And when does the new girl come in?" Amédée asked.

"In an hour, presumably."

He opened the cupboard doors and heaved a big sigh.

"What the fuck is up with him? He hasn't sent in the orders, did you see?"

I nodded.

"We're going to be in deep shit, up the creek!"

Then once he was done fortifying himself he headed back toward the kitchen, he turned on the radio and opened the pass-through with a big clack.

Good old Amédée, sometimes he invited me up to his place for a visit. I'd done the same for him but apparently it wasn't so much to his liking, because I'm really alone these days, like an old bachelor barman, whereas he shares his apartment in Saint-Denis with a bunch of friends who are always coming and going, and he has some very pretty cousins too, they love to laugh, some of them have husky voices and others high-pitched, they dance at the drop of a hat, on Sunday, once lunch is over. When you see them with their kids in the streets, or at the supermarket, or in the park if the weather's good, you tell yourself that happiness is a very common thing, and easy to come by, for Paris's Africans.

Madeleine came in with her hands in her raincoat pockets. She'd taken great pains with her makeup, her lips were redder, and she was wearing less base, I thought. She looked around, there was a little lull at my bar, the boss's wife still hadn't shown. We gave each other a peck on the cheek, she was already one of the staff. When I die I'll be replaced just like that.

"How's everything? It didn't take you too long?"

I often tell myself that, it doesn't bother me, really.

"I'm doing fine, Pierrounet. The bosses aren't here?"

She didn't wait for an answer. She took off her raincoat and hung it on the door in back, she lit a cigarette, and without having to ask I made her her first espresso. She smiled at me.

"Pierrot, you don't even seem to care!"

"You want some milk?"

She nodded.

"I guess they're having a spat, huh? Well, the bloom went off that rose a long time ago."

The rain was starting up again, and now people were hurrying along between the underpass and the pedestrian street.

"Yes, a long time ago," she said again, "you can tell right away. Ah, men!"

She smiled sadly toward the rain. This must all have seemed a long way from Colonel-Fabien. Then no, she stopped smiling. I made a face like I had no idea, and in a sense it was true.

"We'll never manage all by ourselves, thirty-two set-ups, there's just no way!"

I gave the bar a good wipe with the mop rag to erase what she'd said, then I told her, "Yes, we will, Madeleine, it won't be any worse than yesterday, don't you worry."

"What a grind, Pierrounet!"

She put out her cigarette and went to have a good yell with the cook, she showed him her burned hand, but just before that they'd said hello with a kiss on the cheek. Good old Amédée. It was going to be another hard day in the salt mines.

Just before noon the boss's wife came downstairs at last. She'd carefully made herself up to cover the damage of the night before. "Pierre, how are you doing?" "Fine, and you?" She must have done a lot of crying, but she manned the cash register as if things were perfectly normal. I was having to be everywhere at once, this far from a breakdown. At one point I saw Amédée coming out of his kitchen to go see the boss's wife. He silently held out a little stack of papers, she gestured that she understood, he'd written up the orders. Le Cercle was packed, it was almost like they were doing it on purpose, no way we could keep this up for long, especially with Madeleine from Colonel-Fabien, who might decide at any moment it wasn't worth sticking around, you never know. Pierrot my friend, I said to myself, and then I didn't finish the sentence in my head because we really were swamped. At two-thirty I had a quick bite, I hadn't even once glanced out toward the street, where you can always see life going by, along with a wicked draft now and then. Madeleine tended the bar in the meantime, two or three customers asked if I'd heard anything from him, and I said "He's sick, but he'll be back on his feet in no time."

 "It's that time of year."

The boss's wife gave me a look every time, that day Amédée didn't even rib the waitress, we really had too much to do, I never heard one curse from the pass-through. Things were looking bad. I finished my lamb chop with green beans and went over to see her, she was standing there lost in a fog with her eyes glued to the Casio.

"Ma'am, we've got to do something, we can't last another day without him."

She looked at me like she didn't understand.

"He didn't call you?"

"No, Pierre, he didn't even call me. It's not right, it's not right."

She mumbled a few other things I couldn't hear. So I turned all that over in my head, and I asked her:

"Could you give me the keys to the Audi?"

She really seemed very alone just then. She let her gaze wander all around the room, and then she went back to staring at the cash register like it was *The Young and the Restless* or some other soap opera.

"The keys to the Audi? Why? Wait, Pierre, I'll go get them, they must be upstairs."

"OK, thanks."

She didn't want to come with me. I was a little perturbed to see her head back to the cash register, staring off into space, Madeleine had agreed to look after the bar. On my way out I saw the young man in black coming in, and I smiled at him without meaning to, how much longer was he going to keep hanging around Le Cercle, anyway? There were dead leaves on the car again, she was parked on the Avenue de la Marne. I picked them off and drove away, I really should save up and buy myself a car someday, when I get too worn out. I'd left my old one behind when I left my last girlfriend, Jacqueline, and the apartment we lived in. We'd bought that car together, we'd taken out a little loan for the purpose. We also took little vacations together, never more than a week. We toured the châteaux of the Loire, where I was thoroughly bored, and then once in August we rented a place in the country near Dieppe. I wanted to see the beach again, and its pebbles, the first one I'd been to with my new foster family.

I never explained all that to Jacqueline. We'd even made some more distant plans, we'd bought the Michelin guide to Italy, but just then I got scared of the new life spreading out in front of us, and I left her before we could go. Sometimes on Sundays we went for aimless little drives here and there, through the forests around Paris, or along the valley of the Chevreuse, or to Fontainebleau. It must be wonderful around there right now, with the fallen leaves. Why was I thinking of that? I drove through the little streets of Asnières, and when I reached Gennevilliers I took the four-lane toward Eugène-Varlin and the big housing projects, that's where Sabrina lived. I had no trouble finding a parking place under the gray skies, there's construction going on everywhere, walled-off work sites in an unholy mess, with nobody working, it can go on like that here for years at a time. Young guys hang around in the streets, talking loudly about the same things people talk about everywhere else. It's only their voices that change, to tell the truth. Women with baby carriages and plastic bags from the big Carrefour supermarket in Gennevilliers.

I looked at the mailboxes and found Sabrina's name, I couldn't remember what floor she lived on. It felt pretty grim in there, so close to my tidy little suburb, kind of like another world. I rang at her door. There was noise coming from every floor, music, dogs waiting for walk-time, and then the TV in Sabrina's apartment.

"Why, Pierre! Come in!" She was wearing a bathrobe. "What are you doing here?" Her hair was undone, and her eyes were a little too red, she really did have the flu. "Don't get too close, or I'll give you this bug I've got!"

She stood aside to let me in. There were bottles of medicine on her table, she'd set up the ironing board in front of the TV.

"You should have let me know you were coming, I would have straightened up."

I told Sabrina I was just in the neighborhood and thought I'd stop by, the boss had been gone for two days and we hadn't heard a thing from him. Her eyes got wide.

"Oh really? What's up with him?"

She gave a big cough, tears came to her eyes.

"Oh, this flu. I was just about to make some tea, like a cup?"

"Yes, thanks."

She'd taped up her kids' drawings on the wall by the TV, all marked with the dates, and sometimes a few words too, in red, blue, or green. Sabrina was in all sorts of bright colors, a huge sun was shining. It was quiet here, and I would gladly have stuck around a while myself, I could well understand how the boss might fall in love with that girl. And as a matter of fact, Pierrot, I said to myself, but those are just stupid little ideas that come into my head now and then, because I'm alone, and because most of the time I have nothing in front of me but the same old barman's day, and how much longer is that going to last? And then in the evening, at night, that stupid dream that keeps waking me up. She came back with a tray, she had some little cakes on a plate next to the tea. That was very sweet of her, I thought.

"Here, sit down. How are you getting along without him?"

"We're managing. But it can't go on like this. There's a new girl to replace you, she's already sick of the whole thing. You don't know where he is?"

She looked me straight in the eyes.

"I have no idea, Pierre."

We looked at each other like that, and then her pretty smile faded a little, and suddenly I got it, if you don't mind my saying.

"I've had to wait for him too, you know."

"You didn't see him, he didn't even call you?"

She pulled out her handkerchief.

"Excuse me."

I looked around the room like an idiot, maybe there was something to see over by the ironing board. Sabrina had a lot of work to do. I recognized the little boy's clothes, and the girl's colorful dresses. The sky was brighter here, because of the height of the building. Sometimes the sky must even have been a little too bright. It made me think of before, long before, when I wasn't a barman but a fireman, an explorer, a soldier, and a soccer player, a long way from Le Cercle, the bright sky I had inside me, and above me, before the apartment blocks where I grew up. She went into the next room, which must have been her bedroom, and when she came back she sat down on a chair facing me. We drank our tea without a word. Now and then we gave each other a smile. She talked about him a little. My beloved boss. They'd been seeing each other for two years, every chance they got. It was love at first sight, that's what it was. He'd taken her to England once, and then at one point they'd run off to Saint-Malo. He loved Saint-Malo. "Oh really?" At first he was sincere, his marriage wasn't what it used to be, but it hadn't taken her long to figure it out. "Figure what out?" I understood too, she didn't really have to answer.

"What are you going to do, Sabrina?"

She looked around, glanced toward the ironing board, and then she smiled at me, looking at her watch.

"Oh dear, I've got to go pick up the kids at school! I completely lost track of the time! My little girl gets out in ten minutes."

I stood up with her, I put my raincoat back on.

"Don't worry about me, Pierre, I've been around the block, you know. Will you get the elevator? I'll be right there."

We parted ways eight floors below. Sabrina had a laugh in her eyes.

"You'll keep me posted, right, Pierre?"

"Yes, of course, Sabrina. Give the kids a kiss for me."

"By the way, they call you Pierrounet, did you know that?"

She laughed as she was turning away, now she had tears in her eyes. I watched her walk off in her high heels, they'd been clattering around Le Cercle for more than two years now, and as she walked she put on her lipstick so she'd be beautiful like the women in the pictures on the walls. When she was finished she gave me a little wave, without turning around.

Pierrot my friend, I said to myself, and this time it must have been something very important, but I didn't get a chance to say anything because there were some teenagers gathered around the boss's wife's Audi, so what can you do, I went over to see.

"What year is she, m'sieur?"

"You weren't even born yet, my boy."

"How 'bout a ride?"

"Some other time, I'm in a hurry."

"Really? When? You live around here, m'sieur?"

"Yes, and where's your school?"

"On Gabriel-Péri, we didn't have school today, m'sieur. They threw us out for three days."

They all had a good laugh and went on to the next car. I drove away wondering various things, it looked bad this time, was there anything else I could do? I wandered around till it got dark. There are a lot of cafés, and after a while I decided I'd had enough. I went back to Le Cercle, the boss's wife was there waiting for me, looking like she'd never budged from the cash register. Madeleine gave me a dirty look and I raised my arms toward the sky, I told her I was sorry but, you know, what could I do?

"You could have called and let us know," she answered. "Oh, I've had it with this place."

She left right away, without even telling me who'd paid and who hadn't at the bar, but she still gave me a goodbye peck on the cheek.

"Have a good evening, my beauty."

"Not likely, I'm completely done in."

She made a face, looking at the boss's wife, who visibly didn't give a damn about any of this just then. Madeleine crossed the street, the collar of her raincoat was turned up, she stopped at the newsstand to buy a magazine. She headed into the underpass. Too bad, I would have been very happy to chat with her a while longer. There was a big crowd in the café across the street. And then, not long after that, you could see tiny raindrops falling through the mist under the light by the newsstand, like little brushstrokes.

I told the boss's wife he hadn't been there, and he wasn't in any of the cafés I thought likely. She pulled herself together and thanked the barman, which wasn't really her style, as long as I've known her. We had a few customers, not many, it was almost like they'd all got together and decided to stay away. They must have thought something was missing without the boss around, or who knows what. But that was fine by me, at that point I wasn't up to any more work. I went to the bathroom. Then I headed back to my post till seven o'clock. The boss's wife was sitting at a table in back chatting with a friend of hers, Marianne Crège, who runs the hair salon on Maurice-Bokanovski. Now and then she smiled through her gloom, which goes to show, Pierrot my friend, but then I made a U-turn in my head, I just wanted to go home. I went over to see them.

"What about the orders, how are you going to handle that?"

"I'll see to it, Pierre, Amédée wrote up the list for me."

So I said OK, gave her back the keys to the Audi, and found myself outside. I crossed the pedestrian street and set off for the bus stop. I made myself some instant soup and didn't touch Monsieur Primo Levi. If this is a man, I said to myself. If this is a life, Pierrot, yawning. We kept it up like that for another two days, the boss's wife was doing better, I thought, but she wasn't really there, still not a word from him. And then it was Sunday, an extra-beautiful Sunday in the suburbs of Paris.

# III

I lazed around with Primo Levi's book till nine in the morning, and then I saw to myself. I took a long hot shower, and I didn't do any singing, but still it was nice. I went to buy groceries for my neighbor on the third floor, and I brought her her newspaper. For fifty years she's read *L'Humanité dimanche* every week. She's a railway-worker's widow, beyond that I don't know much. I rounded out the morning with some housekeeping, I was happy to be at home. I ran the vacuum cleaner and scrubbed my bathtub. I washed my windows, it was high time, what with all the rain we'd been having. After that I peeled the vegetables I'd bought at this morning's market to make different soups, I used to eat soup every night back when I lived with my foster mother in Clichy. It was a beautiful afternoon, not a cloud in the sky, even if the temperature had fallen a little. But that didn't stop me from going and twiddling my thumbs outside, I went for a walk along the banks of the Seine, just to make sure nothing had changed, in the end. I'm a lover of rivers, like my mother before me. No surprise there, I grew up by the Seine, in Clichy. Some evenings in springtime the two of us would go for a stroll on the banks, and she'd meet up with her friends. When did they take the benches away? And then I called Roger. He was in fine fettle, he told me. His new girlfriend had gone to Sens, she had family there, and he hadn't gone along. Still a bit early for introductions, he thought. He'd spent the morning at work, he was stuck behind his bar at Le Voltigeur till almost two in the afternoon, a nap was the first thing on his agenda. We agreed to meet on the Place Voltaire, we showed up at the same time and spent an hour together, thirty years we've been seeing each other. We talk about whatever comes into our heads, we catch up on each other's lives. Ever since he met Muriel he's been seeing everything through rose-colored glasses, evidently she'd really got under his skin. I smiled in my head, because I'd seen Muriel and I had my doubts about her. It was nice sitting there on the Place Voltaire. I stopped myself from telling him there was always some Muriel getting under his skin ever since he began living alone, and things were picking up speed.

"And what about you, Pierrot?"

"What do you mean, what about me Pierrot? Oh, me? Me?"

Me, nothing, no love in sight. Maybe that was all over and done with now. Then I told him about my beloved boss's disappearance. He'd already heard, news travels fast from one café to another.

"I imagine there's a skirt involved?"

"No, that's not how it seems to me."

"You sure? What, does he have debts or something?"

"I don't think so."

No, his wife hadn't gone to the cops. She said she wanted to wait a while longer. "Well now, that's funny." He looked over toward the Place Voltaire, which is one of the ugliest squares in my suburb, but I've spent some of the finest times of my life there, so that's how it is.

"Maybe she doesn't want to know," Roger said, just making conversation.

"What have you got planned for tonight?"

"Not a thing."

"You want to go to dinner?"

That was OK with him, but not too late, his girlfriend was getting in at ten past midnight and he wanted to meet her at the station. He didn't have to work tomorrow. And had my friend Roger got under her skin? We went for a little walk, we had a very nice Sunday.

We went back to a bar that was once a favorite haunt of mine, ten years ago or so, and there too they asked me for news of my boss. I said "I've got nothing to tell you," and inside me I missed the old-school approach, which is to serve drinks without saying a word, but I was probably imagining things. In any case, with this kind of work you have to learn as you go. I finally decided he was happy wherever he was, and Roger nodded, "If you say so, Pierrot." We drank a beer, and then we said why not, we'd be the evening's first customers at the Kabyle's place. It was as good as it could be at that price, and he at least didn't give a damn about my boss, although we were still treated to the free apéritif, with a *couscous royal* for both of us, and a bottle of Boulaouane, a little too cold for my tastes. It was my turn to pay. We didn't say much as we ate, we like it that way. Afterwards we talked about my dream, and then, as the waiter was giving me back my debit card, I had a sudden illumination.

"What's the matter with you?" Roger asked.

"Nothing, nothing."

"It's not the bill, I hope?"

Good old Roger, he could be a dope too, just like me. It's not nothing to be two friends, in any case.

"I think I know where my boss must be."

"Oh, so that's it," Roger shrugged. "This thing's really shaken you up, hasn't it? And where might he be, in your opinion?"

I finished the Boulaouane, it had finally warmed up, and as always it made me think of my first detox treatment, a year after my divorce. Then I told my pal my idea, he must have gone to see his daughter in England.

"Ah," Roger said. "And you don't think she would have called her mother?"

But I was sure all the same, so that was that.

"If you want my opinion, Pierrot, you're taking all this too much to heart." He looked at his watch. "Well, I've got to be moving on, things to do. Drive you home?"

We shook Slimane's hand, he's a very decent guy too, come to mention it.

After all these years as a barman, everyone I know's in my own line of work. My friend Roger, my friend Pierrot, and then the others. They come and go, for the most part. Let the world turn around us, beyond our spotless bars, in the end every day will be carefully wiped away to make room for the next. That's why I make myself watch the late-night news on Channel 3, you can't just forget everything, after all. I promised myself I wouldn't drink any more wine till next week, if I happened to have dinner out somewhere. I never drink wine at home anymore. Roger was still a close friend, even with all those Muriels getting under his skin. And what about me? I thought vaguely about the student girl on the sixth floor, but I bet that'd be a very bad idea. I did the laundry, my mother always did her washing on Sunday morning, for me it was Sunday night. I hung out my white shirts on the curtain rod in the shower, I got out my space heater to make sure they'd be nice and dry the next morning. I like those moments of my life, and at the same time I'm afraid of them, because sometimes, with one thing leading to another, I forget that I'm a fifty-six-year-old guy, and then I start asking myself questions. I remember my past, more than forty years ago.

It was ten o'clock at night when the boss's wife phoned. She'd called Amédée and Madeleine before me. She'd decided to close the café for a while, take some time to think things over, and then maybe she'd be going to England, she'd phoned her daughter, who was living there, as I knew. "Yes, ma'am."

I felt very tired all of a sudden, I sat down on the bed, my shoulders weighed ten tons, I was completely exhausted. I really had no desire to hang up my apron.

"It's just a week, Pierre, it'll be over before you know it!"

"If you say so," I answered. "You know, this is going to be great news for the people at La Rotonde."

She cleared her throat, she was hoarse from too many cigarettes, probably. She said "I know, Pierre," which meant shut up.

"You think that's where he is?"

"I don't have the slightest idea. Look, I've got to go. I'll keep you posted. By the way, the deliveries will be coming on Tuesday, if you could go deal with them."

"Yes, fine, if you like."

"The checks are in the cash register, behind the coins. Make sure it's all there, you know how they are! Thanks, Pierre."

And then she hung up. I sat down on my bed and waited, then I watched the late-night news on 3. I took another shower to clear my head. I hadn't seen a bit of whatever was going on in the world. This would give me a chance to take care of some things that had been on my mind for a few months. I had to go through my papers, I've been working since I was nineteen but I never knew just how many trimesters I had left before my pension kicked in, because some years there'd been gaps of various lengths. Also, I could finally go to the dentist and get that tooth pulled. I'd already cancelled twice.

When I got out of the shower I set about dealing with the ravages of time, if you'll pardon the expression. The hairs in my ears, the hairs in my nose, and then – although here there's not much you can do – I put on my Nivea. I have a sort of gray and splotchy complexion, like so many others in my line of work. I even tried to masturbate, as a special treat, but I didn't go through to the end. I couldn't find the right picture. That depressed me vaguely, but anyway. I went to bed. Monsieur Primo Levi was waiting in vain beside the alarm clock on my nightstand. I'd brought it here from my mother's, along with all the photos and souvenirs I could manage. The rest I'd tossed out or given to her neighbors. I had my bad dream about the dead leaves in the café, which woke me up at three. I waited for morning to come. What was I going to do, if . . . ? This was some kind of number he'd done on us. Now and then a dull white gleam ran over the ceiling, I'd had it repainted last spring. I nodded off again, but I didn't like what was waiting for me behind my closed eyelids. There were more dead leaves, and women's bodies, and then, with my eyes open now, my mother when I was ten, when I was adopted, and locked doors. And so, at seven in the morning, I was ready to go.

I made the trip on foot. La Rotonde was already open, and as usual I spotted some of Le Cercle's old regulars, side by side with the new ones. Do you ever really meet anyone face to face in a café? I gave the boss there a nod, he reminds me of my own boss, back when he was around. Every morning and evening you can see him out walking a big Irish setter. I hear he goes hunting in the Sologne, he had a house built down there. His business is booming. He's already come calling, very casually, in hopes of worming some info out of me. But I'm from the old school, so a fat lot of good that'll do him, if you don't mind my saying. I turned on the lights and gave the bar another good wipe, because that's how I've started my day for as long as I've been at this job. I put my mop rag in its usual place, and then I fixed myself a cup of coffee. I could see people looking my way, and a lot of fast-moving feet in fancy polished shoes, and some blue-jeaned legs with sneakers, and then the shuffling misshapen boots of the vagrants who wander the streets around here in spite of the city's best efforts and the good people of the employment agency. I cranked the shutter all the way up when ten o'clock came around. The sky was clear and blue overhead, and grayish over toward the Seine, above the train tracks. I closed the door and locked it again. But that was no good, people kept coming and peering in with their hands cupped around their eyes, what would they think? I decided to put up a little sign to make them stop. Where was I going to find paper around here? Pierrot, my friend. I took Amédée's notepad, the one he uses to write down his orders. "Closed due to a disappearance." That seemed a bit indiscreet, I told myself. So I wrote "Closed for a week" in big capital letters, and I thought that was very good. I taped up my sign inside the glass door, and, I'm not kidding, in the space of two hours I counted at least a hundred pairs of eyes that came along to give it a look, and also to stare inside the café, where I was.

I even saw the young man in black. He read my sign and shrugged, saying something out loud to himself, and heading for the café across the street, obviously. I hung around till twelve-thirty, I was about to leave for my appointment to find out how many trimesters I have left when I spotted Amédée. He was wearing a yellow boubou, with a sort of Afro bonnet on his head, and a pretty cousin I'd never seen before on his arm. He chuckled when he saw me, and he was still chuckling when I knelt down to open the lock.

"Hey, Amédée, how are you doing?"

"You taking over for the boss, Pierrot?"

He introduced his friend, she gave me a peck on both cheeks, and they stayed for a while to drink a beer. "What a mess," Amédée said, "I never thought I'd see such a thing." His only question was:

"What'll you do if he doesn't come back, Pierrot?"

"They said next week, Amédée."

"You think it's true?"

He didn't look a bit like the Banania man when he said that.

"Nothing to worry about, Amédée. They can't very well just let it all go, can they?"

And in any case he was a very good cook, certainly much better than the one in Le Rapide, at Quatre-Routes, where I went for lunch once those two had gone on their way. The daily special set me back ten euros, I wanted someplace not too close to Le Cercle, for discretion's sake. I was a fool, I told myself, I would have been better off eating at home, but as a matter of fact no. I took a Paris train and got off at Saint-Lazare, then waited in line to see about this trimester business. Social Security had a whole big building by the Place de l'Europe, the land of offices, the easy life. The secretary explained the new laws that had gone into effect, they'd probably be changing before long, I had a little trouble following it all. I just wanted to know where I stood, and if I was going to end up in the soup line anytime soon. She punched some keys on her computer, pushing her glasses up on top of her head. I wasn't far from a full pension, but I wasn't quite there yet. And then the most important thing was that I was missing all sorts of important papers I'd be needing for my work history, my pay stubs were all out of order, my retirement account statements, I'd gone through some hard patches, and

I'd left them scattered around here and there. I haven't always been the most conscientious person around, but all in all, when I left, it seemed like things were going to work out OK. Still, it was a real relief to get away from there, to take the train back in the other direction with the office workers, the saleswomen, and the students. Night was falling by five-thirty now, and across the Seine I could see headlights all the way to the skyscrapers at La Défense, everything was nicely lit up, and in the water the sky looked brighter than it actually was.

In the train people were reading their newspapers, staring at nothing at all through the windows, fingering their cellphones right up to the very last minute of a very hard day, or who knows what. I walked by Le Cercle, it was turning cold now, and I wondered if there was anything more I could do. Probably not. I ended up going inside anyway. I sat on the corner barstool for a while, and then I went home, still on foot, in hopes of wearing myself out a little.

Two days later I went to the dentist's, which hurt like hell, then in the afternoon I went to let the delivery men in. So now everything was ready to go, we could start up again. I left a message on the boss's wife's cellphone. I said "The deliveries came, everything's in good shape, also Amédée's getting worried. Incidentally, I haven't heard a thing from the new girl." I hung up, that was that.

I realized people were starting to talk in the neighborhood. The folks across the street were making up stories, the guy in the newsstand where I went for my paper was asking me "Is it true?" Rumors were flying around the Asnières station.

"What's going on in that café of yours?"

"Nothing at all, as you see."

"They're not having work done?"

"No, they're not doing a thing."

It was already Thursday, and for two nights I'd slept straight through, like a fifty-six-year-old baby who's been paying into Social Security for thirty-eight years, give or take. Funny-looking pay stubs we used to have. I'd worked in places I could hardly even remember. I'd spent six months in the café across the street, for example, twenty-two years ago, and I had absolutely no memory of it. Or was I just too drunk that year? I'd run around with a lot of women when I was younger, before and after my divorce, and I'd worked in Paris bars a week at a time. I'd even done a season at a vacation club in Agadir because of a love affair that hadn't worked out, a woman from Bois-Colombes, I wanted to marry her. I spread out my whole life on two tables in the back of the dining room. I was making seventy francs a month when I started out. Sorting through all that brought back a good chunk of my life, people's faces, customers I got on with, and some I didn't, and women too, bars and addresses that left big blank spots in my head. Where did all the time go? You don't know, Pierrot? Le Cercle would probably be my last bar, to tell the truth. Jacqueline Serradura will have been my last girlfriend. A few weeks after I ran out on her I realized I could never replace her. And then after that I wasn't so sure. But anyway. Strange feeling, having all that laid out in front of you, and not seeing anything more to come. Still, I wasn't dead yet. Two or three times I nodded off over my pile of papers, and when I woke up I went right back to it. From some years my pay stubs were clean and orderly, other years they were one hell of a mess, wine stains, smudges, little blots of whatever. I aged a lot, watching over that empty café.

Now and then the phone rang, I kept hoping it would be them, this whole thing had dirty trick written all over it now that I thought of it. I got one wrong number, then somebody who wanted to reserve a table for ten, and twice there was no one on the other end, not quite what I had in mind. Once I was done sorting through my trimesters, I did a few crossword puzzles. I also had a chance to finish that Primo Levi book, he'd ended up throwing himself down the stairwell in his apartment building, he'd seen too much. Would he have been interested in other guys of no particular interest, would he have deigned to talk to someone like me? I missed having the young man in black around, it would have been nice to talk all this over with him, maybe he knew more about it than I did? I wiped down the counter one last time before I left that evening, then I lowered the shutter. I still had thirteen and a half trimesters to go before I was eligible for the full pension and my supplemental retirement. I'd managed pretty well in my life, really.

One night I called Sabrina, she was feeling better now. I told her they'd both ended up disappearing, but she was only half listening. It was obvious she didn't know much about any of this. What she did know she must have preferred to keep to herself.

"Don't worry, Pierrounet, you can always come eat at my place!"

She laughed, I heard her children in the background, for them everything was fine, in a way, everything was just fine in her suburban housing project. I was smiling like an idiot when I hung up. In the end I hadn't managed that well, actually. It'd take me another whole lifetime to make it right.

On Friday I came to Le Cercle later than usual. I didn't set off first thing because I was busy giving my two-room apartment in Les Grésillons a good clean. I stopped by the newsstand on my way in, I've always got on well with Monsieur Akilami, that's the guy's name, he's done a lot of traveling compared to most people around here, they have their few weeks' paid vacation and that's it, usually.

"So I suppose you're out of work, my poor friend?"

He really wanted to know what was up.

"Yeah, laid off, it would seem."

"You worked long enough for a pension?"

"Don't know. We'll see."

So, along with *Le Parisien*, I got the paper where they print job listings for my line of work, which is serving drinks to people who pass through your café for ten minutes or an hour, or as long as it takes to eat a meal. They're your equals, and often they'll leave you a tip on their way out, but whatever they've left hanging in their lives hasn't budged a bit. Some of them will come back to see you again and again, year after year. Pierrot my friend, you would have made a great poet. A few trimesters short of your full pension, you could have thrown yourself down the stairwell, with Monsieur Primo Levi's paperback clasped in your scrawny arms. Of course, you only live on the third floor, so you probably would have wound up with nothing more than a broken leg, or a twisted ankle, or a cracked-up coccyx, or a dislocated knee, but that's certain death in your business, no legs, no job. There was plenty of work to be had, from what I'd seen in that paper. I wouldn't be the youngest applicant for any of those jobs, of course. But on the other hand, I'd be the only one capable of watching over a café closed for no apparent reason, and that was where my meditations on the meaning of my life stood when the telephone rang. It made a lot of noise in the empty café. This time I knew the voice on the other end of the line. I could hear his wife in the background, I even got the feeling they weren't alone. I didn't have anything to say about it. I wasn't even all that surprised, in the end. It had come over him like a sudden urge to pee, I told myself, but in fact no, ever since his daughter went away, and, I realized later, ever since the end of his fling with Sabrina, his mind was made up. He didn't dare breathe a word of it to his wife, who'd been following after him for so long. End result: we were all out on our asses.

"For Christ's sake, boss, did you ever stop to think about us, about Amédée, about me?"

He didn't answer, which meant that he didn't give a damn, more or less. Was it because I'd spent eight whole days on that trimester stuff that this was hitting me so hard? I really hadn't seen it coming at all, to tell the truth. He'd been traveling here and there with his wife, visiting cafés that were looking for new management, they were calling from Saint-Malo.

"God damn it, we don't live in Saint-Malo! Fifteen years I've been here in Les Grésillons!"

I'd have to check over the paystubs from my salad days, but actually that didn't tempt me much. We hung up, me first, he wanted me to break the news to Amédée, and I said "No, absolutely not, out of the question, don't waste your breath, the answer's no. That's for you to deal with." He'd found a buyer.

"See you at the labor tribunal."

Some nerve he had, and his wife too, all of a sudden I was sorry he hadn't disappeared for real. I let out a silent howl in the empty café. After that I looked out the window. The trees weren't completely bare. Some of the sycamores that were pruned too short had a few tiny leaves left, still green, they hadn't figured things out yet. All the branches around them were black, the mournful majority, I thought. I'd spent thirty-three trimesters in this café, two of them on disability. Fuck. Pierrot my friend, I said to myself. And this time I did just what he wanted, because at that moment he really was my friend.

I opened the café up for business. I turned on the fluorescent lights over the bar, and even in the dining room. It was six o'clock in the evening. I took down my little sign, then hurried back behind the bar and waited. It wasn't ten minutes before they started show-ing up. But they all had the usual look on their faces, they gave me their orders just like they always did. It was good hard work. I served free round after free round, it was the apéritif hour. By seven there were a good twenty-odd customers in the bar, and then Amédée came in, wearing coveralls. We shook hands, and he asked me straight off if I'd heard the news? I said yes, he'd called me earlier.

"What'll it be, my friend?"

It was a lovely evening. At one point I saw the young man in black coming out of the underpass, I waved him over and he pointed at his chest with one finger to be sure I meant him. Finally he came in.

"I'm celebrating my last day, I'd like to buy you a drink, what do you say?"

He gave me an uncomfortable grin and said:

"Oh, I see, great, can I have a kir, please?"

"Right you are."

Everyone was talking to everyone, nothing loosens the tongue like a free drink, if you don't mind my saying. Amédée came behind the bar to give me a hand, I'd done a lot of hard work in my life. Then they started to leave, in dribs and drabs. With the kid, I drank to Primo Levi's good health. "Oh, you know about him?" I said "Yes, I read his book, you were the one who put me on to him, I bought *Pierrot mon ami* too, I'll read that one soon." So then he was happy to drink another kir in our company.

Amédée was managing nicely, I thought. He got a call on his cellphone, I couldn't hear above the din, but ten minutes later three of his pretty cousins showed up at Le Cercle. We hung around for another hour or so. The uncertain types only nodded when I told them "No, you don't owe me a thing, it's free."

Others said "Thanks, what a nice idea, have a good evening Pierrot, happy retirement," they even left me a tip. We closed up at nine-thirty. The cousins were sitting in the dining room with glasses of Coke and Perrier, and when the last customer left they came and stood at the bar, quite a party we'd thrown together. I had a chat with Amédée. What was he going to do now? He shrugged. He'd wait and see what the new owners had to say, but he really didn't know. There was plenty of work around, in any case. One of the three cousins was particularly pretty, which didn't stop her smiling at us and throwing him longing glances and all that, so there you are. "What about you, Pierrot, you given it any thought?" I didn't answer the cook. But he really wanted to know.

"I'm not sure, Amédée. I've been through a lot, but this sort of thing's never happened to me. I'll go around and talk to some people I know, I'll do some filling in for special occasions, I'll see."

We had one last drink. His cousins were eager to be on their way. "Ready to go, Amédée?" We shook hands.

"We'll keep in touch, right, Pierrot?"

"Yes, of course."

"He said we'd be paid till the end of the month. You believe him?"

I nodded. I didn't tell Amédée. I was very happy to get three pairs of pecks on the cheek. The prettiest cousin had an old blue Ford, she went off to get it from where it was parked on the Avenue de la Marne, they all climbed in, and I watched them drive away. Now I was alone.

I wiped down the counter, turned off the taps, and started the bar dishwasher, I wanted to leave everything very clean, very orderly, just like nothing had happened. This would be yet another place in my life, but I told myself that without tears. I didn't want to let myself go. I still had a few trimesters ahead of me. And what else did I have left? I thought of the young man in black, what was he going to make of his life? Would he have the strength for it all? Or maybe he'd quietly while it away reading hundreds of books in a bunch of different bars, and he'd be happy that way. I would have liked to tell him that, but it had come to me too late, obviously. In all this time he'd been coming to waste his days at Le Cercle, I'd never once found a chance for a real conversation with him. Although. Obviously, I'm no Monsieur Primo Levi. I was just a barman, and an out-of-work one to boot, that night. Fuck. I wanted to call Roger so he could give me his thoughts on what might come next, but that could wait, we were supposed to meet a couple of days later in the pizzeria by the town hall in Clichy-Levallois. Maybe we'd go with Muriel. Too bad I haven't had anyone for what would soon be . . . I tried not to count in my head. But it wasn't like the trimesters, it was easier to figure out. Pierrot my friend, I said to myself. I put away the dishes, the cups, yes, three years, soon it will have been three years. My bar was gleaming, clean as a whistle. Then I swept up. It felt good to do that. There was almost no one coming out of the station by the time I was done. I didn't feel like going home to Les Grésillons. I checked again to be sure everything was as it should be, I turned off the lights at the box in the kitchen. I took one last look. Everything was shipshape now, I could leave this place. I took out the trash from behind the bar and left the can on the sidewalk, by the door. Soon everything would be cleared away. I kept the key to Le Cercle in my pocket, I wasn't going to just leave it in the mailbox, you never know. So, Pierrot my friend, what now? Um . . . you mean me? Yes, that's right, you. I took the underpass and headed for track B to wait for the local to Saint-Lazare. There couldn't have been more than ten of us in the last car, and I felt like we were all rushing together toward a big, not completely black hole, but I seemed to be the only one who knew. The trees were pretty to look at, over by the Seine. I had no idea what I was

going to do next, I only knew I wanted to get home to Les Grésillons very late. I got off at Pont-Cardinet and started walking.

I wandered around for a while, and then I went into a café near
Batignolles park. I ordered a beer from a young guy in a white
shirt and sat down by the front window, not too far from the
door. I had another and we talked a little, when you're in the
business you recognize each other. Maybe a barman still served
some purpose, after all? He'd ended up here by chance, and for
the moment it suited him fine. I could see his reflection in the
window, looking out toward the boulevard with his tray under
his arm. He wouldn't keep the change, obviously he didn't want
me to leave him a tip. And that was that. I started back toward
Saint-Lazare to catch the last train home. But the closer I got the
less I liked that idea. In the end, I decided to walk back to Les
Grésillons. All my papers were piled up on my table, and in my
head all the trimesters to come, waiting for me, and all my past. I
took a nice shower, not too hot. It was way too late for the Channel 3 news. I wasn't really up to reading on a night like tonight.
Then I couldn't think of anything else to do, so I went to bed.